BY TENEKA WOODS

Hot August Nights

Wednesday at Noon

A Cruise Away From Crazy (a novella)

A CRUISE AWAY FROM CRAZY

a novella

TENEKA WOODS

A Cruise Away From Crazy is a work of fiction. Names, characters, places, and incidents are products of the author's imagination or are used fictitiously, and any resemblance to actual people, living or dead, or to businesses, companies, events, institutions, or locales is entirely coincidental.

ISBN 978-1-7336787-4-2 (paperback)
ISBN 978-1-7336787-5-9 (ebook)

Cover design: Paper & Sage
Formatting: Polgarus Studio

1

while making plans

I swear if I didn't just close on my lovely tri-level townhouse last month, and if I wasn't afraid of going to jail, I would hop right across this desk and choke a bitch. But, no. I can't afford to lose my job now that I'm obligated to twenty years of mortgage payments. And my brother Petey spends his life in and out of prison, so it's only right that I think about Mama and how my actions would affect her. It makes no sense for two of her three children to be the family's fuck-ups.

My eyes haven't blinked since the superintendent came into my office five minutes ago and dropped a bombshell. My assistance is needed in organizing the Daddy Daughter Dance because Rebecca, the program coordinator, has been granted personal time off as she's under severe stress.

"But I leave for vacation this week. On Thursday, remember?" I said.

"I am aware of that," the superintendent nodded. "And believe me if there was someone else I could put on it I would have, but Nick is helping Marc while Sonya is out. Our hands are tied right now."

"How about Keagan? She was a huge help with the holiday drive."

"There's only so much the intern can do. I'd rather she focus on other projects."

I'm not sure what kind of *severe stress* Rebecca is dealing with, but it sounds like a bunch of bull to me. Hell, I'm under stress too, which is why I worked my tail off the past couple weeks to ensure the priority items on my to-do list were completed so this week would be smooth-sailing. And in three days I will be sailing off on a four-day cruise to Cozumel. It's a little house-warming gift to myself and a much-needed getaway since I have become the designated go-to around here, picking up the slack wherever one of my teammates is lacking. So for this lady to bring her ass in here and tell me something like this right before I'm scheduled to leave is like a double-slap in the face.

"This is such a short notice. I mean… how much do you expect me to be able to do by Wednesday?" I ask, trying to keep my voice neutral.

"I will stick around for an hour or two this afternoon to help you get started, but I have that seminar to attend. There is a binder on Becca's desk. I believe she's already done two of the contracts and insurance verification."

I had my afternoons all mapped out: today I would take my lunch hour and go to the mall to buy two more swimsuits, and see if that sundress I want is on sale. Tomorrow is a facial, mani and pedi. On Wednesday I planned to skip lunch and finish the workday an hour early in order to make it to my hair appointment on time. And I still need to pack.

"I really, really appreciate your hard work and how you're always available, willing to help," she says, standing. "I owe you a special lunch when you return from your vacay."

I get up and close the door when she leaves just so I

can have a few minutes to roll my eyes and cuss in peace.

You're always available.

She's damn right about that, which is the problem.

It's a quarter to eight and I finally shut my computer down. I wave to the security guard on my way out. "See you tomorrow, Joaquin."

"Have a good night, Misses Green," he says.

The mall is only a ten-minute drive away, which means I'll have about an hour to do some shopping.

I pull into a parking spot at Nordstrom because that's where I saw that cute multi-colored stripe maxi dress the last time I visited. I envision myself in it now, the wind catching it as I stroll on the upper decks of the cruise ship.

My cell phone rings in my purse just as I make it to the women's department.

Shaking my head, I reluctantly answer when I see it's my sister calling.

"Hey."

"Millie, what you doing? Can you come pick me up? This damn car just died on me."

I close my eyes and take a deep breath. "Where you at, Tan?"

"Out here off Canal. I just left Sookie house. She did my taxes for me."

"Where is your husband? I'm still at work." I say this because my sister is the last person I would tell that I'm out spending money.

"I thought you get off at six?"

"One of my coworkers is out, so I'm having to do her shit. I'm working late."

"'Til what time?"

"Tan, I'm still in The Woodlands. Where is your husband? Why can't he come and get you?"

"I ain't talking to him right now. His ass didn't even come home last night, so... fuck him."

This cannot be happening. "Sis, y'all are way too old to be going back and forth like this."

She goes quiet, doesn't even bother responding and then I hear her drag on a cigarette.

I don't even bother asking if she has Triple A. "Honestly, I'm not sure how much help I'll be. It's not like I will be able to fix anything. Have you called Mama? Maybe she can send Petey. He can get there faster than I could." I'm basically tiptoeing down the aisles now searching for the dress so she doesn't hear my shoes clacking against the floor.

"She say he in her car. He left early this morning and she ain't seen him since."

A car horn blares in the background.

"Go around! You see I ain't moving, you dumb bitch!"

"Tan, are you in the middle of the street?" I spot the dress and scurry over to the rack. Damn. It's still at regular price. Even though it's a dream I can't rationalize spending that much for it just yet.

"Hell yes. I told you it fell dead. I coasted it as far as it would go."

"Turn your cautious lights on. The last thing you want is for some fool who's not paying attention to fly up and rear-end you."

"Do you really think I would be sitting out here without my flashers on?"

"Are the kids with you?" I ask.

"They at home. Look... can you come or not? 'Cause I can leave this piece of shit right here and catch the bus home with the way I'm feeling."

Tan is ten months younger than me, but she likes to boss me around as if she's the big sister. I want to tell her that in the time it will take me to make it to that part of town she could have taken two round bus trips home, but I hold my tongue instead because I know she's aggravated right now. So I finger the dress one more time before turning away, heading for the exit.

* * *

She's standing under a street lamp post on the sidewalk. I'm not surprised to see a gentleman has come to her rescue. Her hand is on his shoulder, her head snapping back in place from neck-bending laughter I assume as I approach the intersection. She recognizes the headlights on my CX-5 and waves me over as if she saw me first.

"It's about time, sis. Damn. We out here getting ate up by mosquitoes," she says as soon as I exit my vehicle.

"You act like you don't know how far The Woodlands is," I say. The man is standing there grinning, eyeing us as my sister meets me halfway and gives me a hug. I know it's just Tan's way of taking the opportunity to show him what she's working with in her denim jeggings.

"This my sister Millicent," she tells him, and I'm grateful he only nods at me instead of putting his grungy hand out for a shake. "Millie, he say he can pull the car for me. I'm gonna have him take it to Mama's house."

"Why Mama's house? Shouldn't he take it to your house so Darell can see what's wrong with it tomorrow?"

She narrows her eyes at me and I don't know if it's because she hasn't told the man—whatever his name is—that she's married or if it's to remind me she said she's not speaking to my brother-in-law.

"I'm gonna see if Muncho can look at it."

I shrug and get back into my SUV while Grungy Man prepares her car to tow. He tells her to stand as a lookout for oncoming traffic while he attaches the rope.

It is the most agonizingly slow car ride ever.

We finally arrive at Mama's house in what seems like an hour later. I park my car at the curb and hop out to go inside to say hello while Tan and Grungy Man work to maneuver the car into the driveway.

My niece answers the door, practically knocking me down as she wraps her arms around my waist, and I know immediately that she wants something.

"Auntie Millie, will you take me to Wal-Mart? I need a poster board for my project due tomorrow and Daddy still ain't here. I told him last night I needed it and he promised he would buy it today while I was at school and leave it on my bed, but Gigi say he left with the car this morning and he's still not back yet. It's due tomorrow! Please, Auntie?"

"Whoa, Dana. Wait a minute. Take you to Wal-Mart?"

Before I can answer Mama is coming from her bedroom down the hall, asking, "What the hell is going on outside?"

"Hey, Mama," I say. "Tan's car broke down. She said she's going to leave it here until Muncho can check it out tomorrow and see what's wrong."

"The hell she is! How is she just gonna park her shit in my driveway without asking me? She know damn well she ain't getting that car fixed tomorrow."

I just shake my head as Mama storms past me and out to the driveway.

"Say what now, Dana?" I return to my niece who's still hanging on to me like a baby koala on a tree. Except, she's not a baby, but my eleven-year-old twin. I call her my twin because everyone swears she looks more like me than her own mother. But then, people also say me and Petey look alike, so all that really means is that Dana looks like her daddy with her dark chocolate skin, sable eyes, broad nose, and mouth that appears to span the width of her face when she smiles.

“My project is due tomorrow and I need a poster board,” she says again.

“Dana, why would you wait until the last minute to do a project? If it’s due tomorrow that means you’re gonna be up all night trying to get it done.” I glance at my watch. “It’s already nine-thirty. And this is the time you should be in bed, right?”

“Gigi lets me stay up until eleven sometimes if I still got homework to do.”

“Have you tried calling your daddy to find out where he is?”

“He don’t have his cell phone no more,” Dana says.

That tells me all I need to know. I take a deep breath and pray Petey’s just lost track of time and is not out in the streets, back to his old antics. He’s been home only six months after his last three-year stint at the Hunstville Unit for drug possession.

“Go put your shoes on,” I say.

Mama and Tan are making their way back into the house as I sit on the loveseat to wait.

“This man did this as a courtesy,” Tan is saying. “Why would I have him move the car again just because you don’t want it in your driveway, Mama?”

“Because it’s *my* damn driveway and because I know how you are. Tomorrow you’re gonna call me up with an excuse why the car needs to be here for another two days. Then two days is gonna turn into two weeks and so on and so on.”

“No I’m not. As soon as I get off work tomorrow I’ll be over here with Muncho.”

“Then why not just have him haul it over to Muncho’s house?”

Muncho is the neighborhood mechanic who lives six blocks over. We all went to school with him, although he never made it past the tenth grade. But that didn't stop him from using his brains and hands to earn a living. On any given day you can pass by his mama's house to find four cars in the front yard and at least three parked along the curb waiting to be repaired. Petey once told me Muncho can make up to a thousand dollars in one day fixing cars. And Uncle Sam doesn't get to take one cent of it.

Tan doesn't have an answer to Mama's question, so she's just standing there with an annoyed look on her face.

"It better be gone by eight o'clock tomorrow."

"What if he can't fix it in one day?"

"Then it better be gone by eight o'clock Wednesday night." Mama covers her mouth, laughing as Tan slams the door on her way out. "Now see... she wouldn't be pissed off if I wasn't telling the truth. She know damn well she ain't getting that car fixed no time soon."

"I think her and Darell are having problems again," I say.

"Girl, what else is new?" Mama sits on the sofa and crosses her smooth brown legs and suddenly I remember I need to schedule a wax appointment. "If Tan wasn't so damn vindictive...." She laughs again. "Did I tell you Darell called me one day last week?"

"No," I say.

"That poor boy called me up... he said—"

Now she's really laughing, hardly able to get the words out, and then I start laughing because she's laughing.

"He called me and said Tan had cooked some spaghetti *again*. He said, 'Mama, she always cooking spaghetti... we eat spaghetti pretty much every other week!' So, he was sick of it, and told her he wasn't eatin' no damn spaghetti for the rest of the year, and that he had the taste for some beans and franks.... He then went into the kitchen and put on some beans and franks...”

I scoot over on the loveseat as Dana comes to sit beside me with her mini backpack purse on her back, and she starts giggling too, so I know she’s heard this story before.

Mama falls back onto the sofa now, tears trickling down her cheeks. “Millie, he say when he got out of the shower and went to the kitchen to make his plate, Tan had done chopped up his franks and put ’em in the spaghetti!”

All three of us are hollering now.

It takes a few minutes for Mama to calm down. “Wooo,” she finally breathes, shaking her head. “My poor baby. She got it honest. I spoiled that child. I really did. It’s always been her way or no way.”

Of course Petey is back at the house when me and Dana return from Wal-Mart. He apologizes to Dana as soon as she is out of the SUV, telling her he totally forgot about the poster board.

“No worries, Daddy,” she says, and runs into the house to start on her project.

“What’s up, Mill?” He waves at me.

I really should be heading home so I can get ready for work tomorrow, but it’s been a couple of months since I’ve seen my big brother because he’s never here whenever I stop by to visit Mama, so I decide to stay a few minutes and find out what he’s been up to. I turn off the engine and get out.

He hops his tall lanky butt on the hood of Tan’s Oldsmobile. “Mama’s already cussed me out, so I guess you wanna fuss now too, huh?”

“About what?” I say, and stand next to him, leaning my back against the car.

“Being here for Dana.”

"Where were you all day?"

"Shit... looking for work."

"Mm." I cross my arms and ankles. "I was hoping you weren't out doing something crazy..."

"Is that what you think of me?" He shakes his head. "I told you this last time was my last time." He produces a joint out of nowhere and fires it up. After a while he says, "You know it's hard trying to find good work for good pay."

He likes to remind us how hard it is for him to find a job with a felony record. It's the same situation every time he gets out of the pen. Then the three of us (me, Mama, and Tan) find ourselves carrying him until he's able to stand on his own feet. Mama houses and feeds him and lets him use her car to go out and job hunt during the day while she's at work. He calls me to complete online applications for him, when he has to go somewhere on the weekends, and if he needs money. Tan helps out a lot with Dana, keeping her hair braided and taking her in when Mama works extra hours at the hospital.

He says, "That's why I like going straight up to the company, asking to speak directly to the hiring manager because... I believe... even though these companies claim they felony-friendly, I feel like as soon as they see on my application I'm a felon, they throw it out. So... by me going up there to have a conversation with them, they can see me face-to-face and know I'm genuine."

"What about Mr. Kim? Have you tried him?"

Petey lowers his head, chuckling. "C'mon, Mill...."

"At least you'll have *something* until you can find one better."

Mr. Kim is one half of the Korean couple who owns a beauty supply store. They're a felony-friendly business, and known to give opportunities to people in the neighborhood needing a second chance at life. Petey worked for them once before, but Mr. Kim couldn't guarantee him more than twenty-five hours a week, and Petey was sick of hanging wigs and unboxing earrings all day.

"Naw... honestly, I did go and see him though. He ain't got nothing for me."

"I just don't want you getting frustrated and giving up on yourself," I say. "What about your phone? Dana told me it got cut off."

"It'll be back on tomorrow. I did a little bit of work for Mr. Eloy. Got eighty bucks out of it. So don't worry, Mill." Then he wraps his arm around my shoulders and offers me the joint.

"Are you crazy?" I laugh, pushing his hand away. "And have me fail a random at work?"

2

feeling drained

It is wise to live where you work when residing in Houston. The city is so spread out, traffic is a beast, and one can easily spend up to three hours in their vehicle each day commuting to and from work. And yet, knowing all of this, I still chose to purchase my home in Midtown, which is a whole forty-five miles away from the office. I hit the snooze button three too many times this morning and arrived a half-hour late to work. My eyes remained straight-ahead as I walked past the superintendent's office, rationalizing that if I didn't see her then she didn't see me.

I don't like coffee, but right now I need coffee. Only two hours have passed and I'm sleepy as hell. It was around midnight when I made it home last night, another hour before I finally settled into bed. I don't remember exactly what time I fell asleep because my mind wouldn't rest, going over what all I still have to do before Thursday morning.

Damn you, Rebecca. I'm still tripping on the fact she was able to request time off *just because she's stressed.* Where they do that at? Is this a benefit offered outside of one's allotted vacation time? Did I miss something in the employee handbook? I know there's only one person in HR who would give me the inside scoop, and I consider calling her for a second, but then I change my mind. Is it really any of my business why Becca took off work, leaving behind a major commitment for somebody else to pick up? It still won't change the fact that it has to be done. Besides, I know the reason—whatever it may be—won't be worthy enough in my book, so I decide to put my feelings aside for the moment.

"Hey, girl. Did you bring your lunch?"

I look up from my computer. It's Kya from accounting. I really don't feel like hearing a story today. And Kya's always got a story to tell. I've never met her family and friends, but I've heard so much about them I feel as if I know them personally. Her mama, Kathryn, married for the seventh time; she married her third husband twice. Kya's sister (who's really her cousin but Kathryn raised her) is the proud mistress of an airline pilot who flies her all over the world to be with him. If I remember correctly, the pilot's wife has leukemia, and he'd told his mistress he wouldn't dare abandon his wife in her condition. I know about the time Kya's best friend drank too much one night at her company's business retreat and threw up all over the place while giving a presentation the next morning.

Kya knows all about what's going on here in the office too: who's sleeping with whom, who got beef with somebody else, and who is pissed off because they got passed over for a promotion.

I say, "I did, but I'm leaving in about fifteen minutes because I have an appointment. I plan to eat here at my desk when I get back."

"Oh. I was gonna ask if you wanted to come with me to Panera Bread."

"I haven't been there in a while. You know I would join you if I didn't have an appointment."

She invites herself on into the office and takes a seat in the chair. "I heard you were going on vacation this week. Are you doing anything fun?"

I smile at the thought. "Yes. I'm going on a cruise to Mexico."

"Oooh... that sounds like a lot of fun. Who are you going with?"

"Nobody. It's just me."

"Whaaat? Why are you going by yourself?" she asks.

"Why not?" I say. "I just wanna get away for a while. Relax on the beach. Enjoy my own company. Y'know...."

"I could never take a vacation by myself. That's not even a vacation. Who are you gonna talk to? What are you gonna do? Who's gonna take your pictures?" She shakes her head as if it's the most depressing thing she's ever heard.

But I've always been a loner. Aside from Tan, I can count on one hand with a couple fingers left over the number of close friends I've had in my life. While I don't consider myself antisocial, I'm just one of those types of people perfectly content doing things solo. I realize being around others for an extended period of time leaves me feeling drained.

Which is why Thursday morning can't come soon enough because I'm long overdue for some time away.

"Well, maybe you'll meet you somebody. Maybe you'll get you some."

I laugh, shaking my head. "I'm not even thinking about that, Kya. This vacation is all about rest and relaxation."

"Anyway...," Kya whispers, and scoots the chair a little closer to my desk. "You will be the first to know, but guess what?"

"What?" I say.

She cocks her head. "Are you gonna at least *try* to guess, Millicent?"

"Geez, Kya. I don't know. It could be a million things."

"It's about me."

"That's some kind of hint alright." I spend a few seconds thinking of what it could be. Then I lower my voice. "You're leaving?"

She giggles. "No. What makes you think that?"

I shrug, shaking my head.

"I'm having a baby," she grins, and her tongue slides out of her mouth, the tip curves up to meet her top lip as if she's just told me the juiciest secret.

I know she sees the confusion etched across my face because I am certain she referred to the woman she introduced to everyone at the company holiday party as her wife. "Oh," is all I can say because I don't want to say anything that will make me sound as ignorant as I feel.

"And no... we did *not* go to a sperm bank." She laughs. "We care about how our child will look."

I laugh too.

"Our baby was conceived the natural way..."

My eyebrows lift.

"He's our friend. We trust him. And Natalie was there... all three of us in the same bed."

Okay this revelation has gone way beyond what I was expecting. And I'm not sure why Kya felt I needed to know all of these details. Now, I'm not a prude by any means, but this is just TMI, especially from a coworker. But that's how some of these folks are around here. They share everything going on in their personal lives and then wonder why the information they volunteer is later used against them during office gossip and politics.

"Well... congratulations," I say. "I'm happy for you." Glancing at the clock on the computer I realize this is the perfect time for me to make my exit. I tap the keyboard keys to activate my screensaver then retrieve my purse from the desk drawer. “Girl, I gotta go now. I don’t wanna be late for my appointment.”

* * *

I close my eyes, grab my shoulders. Squeezing, massaging the muscles, working my hands all the way up my neck. I lower my head forward, and then slowly move into head rotation exercises. It’s another late night. I’ve been working on this marketing flyer for over an hour now, and I’m beginning to think I should have left this for my PA, Carmen, to do. Instead, I had her assisting with vendor phone calls most of the day, which is my least favorite thing to do because making calls can be so time-consuming. But, between the two of us, we were able to secure the majority of the major vendors needed for the Daddy Daughter Dance.

I get up for a restroom break to stretch my legs and let my mind rest for a few minutes. The office is kinda spooky this late at night because it’s so quiet, and even though I know Joaquin is downstairs, and all visitors must be scanned in by him, I find myself walking briskly through the halls as if somebody’s gonna jump out of one of the offices.

Music is playing when I finally exit the ladies’ room. Luther Vandross. His song ‘Don’t You Know That’ to be exact. Mama played Luther so much when we were kids I practically know all of his songs.

I smile, thinking, what does Joaquin know about Luther? If I had to estimate I’d say Joaquin is no more than twenty-two, twenty-three years old. But I guess that doesn’t matter. Good music is good music at any age.

Maybe he’s come up here to check on me.

I turn the corner and see it’s not Joaquin at all. The first thing I notice is a wide back. A fine wide back. My eyes are fixed on the muscles jerking beneath a black polo shirt as the gentleman fluffs out a trash bag. They travel downward to his black jeans as he bends over and stuffs the can with the bag, pulling and tying the excess with a flourish and quickness so the bag is airtight around the rim.

He returns the can to its place then moves on down to the next office, reaching behind himself for the chain of trash bags hanging from his back pocket. I never imagined there could be a time I'd find watching a man disposing of garbage sexy. But I guess anything can be sexy if the person committing the act is sexy. Those bow legs got me wondering if he rides horses.

Who is he and what is he doing here I wonder. Well, I can clearly see what he's doing here, but it's not often a girl comes across a fine specimen such as this one after hours on the job. Maybe I should hang around until seven on Tuesday nights more often.

I clear my throat to make my presence known so I'm not caught staring like a fool.

He turns, and the frontal view is even better than I anticipated.

I thank his mama for having the foresight to know it was necessary to shape her son's head after birth in the event he decided to shave it in the future, because this is the best bald head I've ever seen.

"Excuse me," I say, hoping the guilt I feel isn't showing all over my face as my eyes rest on his suckable lips.

He immediately reaches for his phone to turn down the music. "I'm sorry," he says, his voice a deep rumble I feel in my own chest. "I didn't know someone would be here. The security guard didn't say anything."

"It's cool," I say. "I just didn't wanna catch you from behind." *Lord, why would I say that?* I try again. "Catch you off guard, I mean."

His smile is infectious, and I'm waiting for him to say something, but he's only looking at me, and now this situation has gone awkward.

I exhale a breath. "Well, my office is the last one on the right. I won't be too much longer," I say, and continue down the hall.

I'm halfway there before I hear another swish of a trash bag.

I ignore the missed call and voicemail from Tan. I'm definitely not answering her right now because I'm determined to email this draft of the Daddy Daughter Dance flyer to our graphics designer before I leave tonight. If she needs something, she's just going to have to call Mama or somebody else. I still haven't had the time to shop for new swimsuits, and I never did get that facial because the mani/pedi took longer than I'd expected. I can just hear her now if I were to return her call... 'Millie, can you spot me such-and-such dollars until I get paid next Friday? Muncho said it's the something-or-other and it's gonna cost xyz....'

But I'm not falling for it. She has a whole working husband at home and she needs to put whatever they're going through aside and take care of her business with her husband's help for once.

"Still here, huh?"

I smile at Sexy Trash Collector. "Yes, unfortunately. Trying to finish this up so it's one less thing I have to complete tomorrow," I say.

"Hey, I hear ya...."

"One of my coworkers is on leave," I ramble on. "So... I'm covering for her. In addition to my own duties...." I cover my mouth to suppress a yawn. "It's been a tough couple of days."

“That’s what I’m dealing with right now,” he says. “One of my employees had to leave unexpectedly. She had to fly back to her country because her mom is really sick.”

“Oh okay—” *Employees huh?*

“Poor lady didn’t have the money to get home, so I went ahead and footed the bill for her flight.”

“Really? That was nice of you.”

“Yeah. To Panama. She’s been gone for about two weeks now. She called a couple days ago to tell me she doesn’t know when she’ll be back. And the lady I had working in her place is out sick, so....” He chuckles. “It’s been a rough couple nights for me, too.”

I’m putting two-and-two together in my head.

He says, “You mind if I take a few minutes to vacuum your office? I’ll be quick so you can get right back to work.”

“Not at all,” I say.

* * *

I activate Bluetooth to return my sister’s call. She’s guaranteed to keep me awake on this long and dark commute home. I ended up leaving the office later than I’d planned because Mr. Sexy Trash Collector and I were involved in a lengthy conversation. His name is Warren J. Proctor, and he’s been providing janitorial services for our office for a year. I told him I’d never seen him before, and he let me know he usually goes to a job site only if there’s an emergency or if he wants to drop in to check on his staff.

He gave me his business card and encouraged me to give him a call if there’s ever a problem with his team’s services.

“Hey, Tan,” I say when she finally picks up the phone. “What’s going on?”

“Hey, sis. I’m glad you called me back.” She sighs

deeply. "The same ol' shit, Millie. It's just the same ol' shit."

And I wait. This will be another venting session. I've been listening to my sister vent about her husband since we were kids. Yes, kids. I was there when she met him—sitting between the two of them to be exact. It was in the eighth grade at Key Middle School where we shared the same Homeroom. He's a Green too, and when the teacher took attendance, she'd call the three of us as if we were one unit: DarellMillicentTangela Green.

I didn't understand what my sister saw in old hook-head Darell in the first place. Me, Mama, and Petey were sure it was just puppy love and wouldn't last beyond middle school. But here they are nineteen years later.

"I just can't do it no more," she is saying, and I can't help rolling my eyes. I would have several hundred thousand in the bank if I had a dollar for every time she's said this.

"How much more can I take? I'm tired of the lying, the fucking around. What am I teaching my daughters? Huh? I been with this man nineteen years. Cleaning, cooking, washing his dirty drawers for fourteen. Fourteen, sis! Wiped his ass when he couldn't wipe it hisself after he broke his arm on that damn motorcycle. That don't count for shit? I mean... how much more can I take? I'm just sick of being in the same gotdamn place. We ain't progressing. What's the point of being in a marriage if you ain't going no damn where?

Babygirl came to me the other day and said she wanted to join the drill team. And do you know what I told her? I told her, 'Rain, you know we can't afford that.' But, then I got pissed off, thinking to myself, 'Why *can't* we afford it?!' I'm sick of not being able to afford shit. Now when my income tax check come in I gotta use that to get the car fixed, and ain't no telling how much that's gonna be. I'm just tired, Millie. Tired of Darell not taking care of shit he's supposed to take care of. I'm tired of his mama always opening her big ass mouth to say something about the type of wife I am, what I need to be doing, and how I need to treat her son..."

As Tan rages on I think back to the day she and Darell got married. We graduated high school in May; they were married in September. It was a beautiful ceremony, held in our granny's backyard. There were only about twenty family members and friends in attendance. Granny fried some chicken and invited her pastor to officiate. I remember thinking, 'I can't believe my sister is getting married. Now she's gonna go off and live her life without me'. Both of them were grinning ear-to-ear like Ches cats that day. Me and Mama cried. Tan got pregnant that night. Mama was just glad they'd waited until after they were married to have babies.

From what I see, I believe they're just tired of each other. They are all each other know. From middle and high school sweethearts, to husband and wife, to young parents. They haven't had the chance to be on their own, find out who they are individually. I know getting married young can work for some people, but others need time to navigate their way through adulthood before they are stable enough mentally and emotionally to invite a partner on the journey.

Tan talks a lot of stuff, but she's done her dirt too. My sister is a major flirt, but I can't say for sure if she's ever cheated on Darell. And like Mama said, she's always been bossy.

But, is what my sister claim worth splitting up her family? They have four girls, and I can't imagine how this will affect my nieces.

When I can finally get a word in I say, “Tan, have you ever thought about going to counseling? I mean... nineteen years is a long time. Maybe y’all just need to sit down and talk to somebody. And I don’t remember y’all ever doing anything alone. Y’all always have the girls with you.”

After a long and quiet moment she says, “Hell, counseling cost money too.”

Mama likes to say I haven’t married yet because witnessing Tan and Darell’s marital woes has turned me off. That may be a little bit true. Honestly, I’ve never gotten much attention from guys. Throughout school Tan was considered the prettiest sister, and I admit she got her natural sex appeal from Mama. Even now, whenever we go out somewhere, Tan gets the attention. I may turn a couple heads, but I’m hardly ever approached. Mama tells me it’s because I don’t appear approachable—that I’ve got this resting bitch face. That might be the case, but that’s just my face. I’m not a bitch at all, although my ex-fiancé would probably say otherwise. It was three years ago when I called off our engagement because I wasn’t feeling the relationship anymore. Since then, it’s been a desert around these parts.

3

a lot going on

"I understand we're in a bind right now with Becca out, but I need a day."

The superintendent is usually in the office by 7:30 every morning, so I called her to plead my case.

"I've been working ten and twelve hour days to get as much done as possible, which hasn't left me any time to pack for my vacation. I am confident my PA can handle things while I'm out today. It would be great if I could work from home."

A small weight is lifted from my shoulders as soon as the call ends, although I could sense she wasn't too happy about my request. But what's the point of having a project assistant if they can't assist with anything? The superintendent needs to have more faith in our PAs and interns. I know mine is the best we have and that's because I trained her well.

I then leave a voicemail for Carmen, telling her to be on the lookout for an email detailing what we have to do today and how I can be reached if she needs me.

I get up to start a load of laundry. At least now I can walk around in my pjs. Maybe I will cook a big breakfast. I can't remember the last time I had a good, sit-down meal before I began the workday. Usually I grab some fast food and eat in front of my computer at the office while checking emails.

It's 12:30 now, which is a good time for me to stop. I need to go to the mall, and then stop by Target for some toiletries, but first I have to call Warren.

I thought I'd put his business card in my purse, but I remember now I slid it into the side pocket of my lunch bag last night.

"Hi, Warren. This is Millicent. How are you?"

"Hey... Millicent. How are you?"

"Doing good. Hey, listen... I'm sorry to bother you—"

"Oh, no, you're not bothering me at all. How are you this morning? Afternoon, I mean."

Do I detect a smile in his voice? Shit, I'm smiling now too. "Doing good," I say again. "Hey, I was just thinking about our conversation last night, and was wondering if you have any positions available."

It takes a few beats before he answers.

"Well, yes, I do as a matter of fact," he says. "Are you looking to change careers?"

I laugh. "No, not for me. I know someone. Well... it's my brother, actually. He's been looking for a while now."

"Oh okay." Warren chuckles. "Well, yeah, tell him to go to our website and apply."

I take a minute to think about how I want to approach this. "Well, see, I have to be honest with you. He has a felony. But I can vouch that he's a hard worker. He's a single dad of an eleven-year-old girl. He's made a few mistakes in life, but he's ready for another chance to get back on track. He's done a little bit of everything: warehouse, retail.... This is not me begging for a handout. But it seems he doesn't have much luck with employers because of his record. So, I wanted to give you a heads-up beforehand. His name is Petey Green."

Warren is quiet, and I imagine he's evaluating the risks. He finally says, "I tell you what... give him my number and tell him to call me."

"Thank you so much," I say.

"I have two positions open. And remember I was telling you about the young lady who went back home? So there might be a third one here pretty soon."

"When's a good time for him to call you?"

"Anytime today before six o'clock would be good."

"I'm gonna call him right now," I say.

"You're leaving tomorrow, aren't you?" Warren asks.

"Yes," I smile. "Can't wait to get the heck away from here!"

"Well... maybe I'll see you tonight. One last time before you go."

My heart drops. "Aww... I'm working from home today."

"Maybe I can see you when you get back then?"

"Sure. We can set that up."

He chuckles. "Give me a call when you get back in town. Have a safe trip," he says.

I hang up and call Petey right away. I'm glad his phone is back in service as he promised it would be. "Petey, I got some good news for you."

"What's up, Mill?"

"Call this guy. His name is Warren Proctor. I told him about you looking for a job, and he said for you to call him. He knows about your felony and everything."

"You serious, Mill?"

"Yep."

"What kinda job is it?"

"He has a janitorial company. They clean office buildings."

"How much they paying?"

"Does it matter? You need a job, fool!"

He laughs. "Hell yeah it matters, sis. It don't make no sense for me to get one if I still ain't earning enough to make a living."

"How much money are you making right now, Petey?"

"What?"

"How much do you bring home every week?"

He chuckles. "I see you talking slick."

"So call him. Right now. He's expecting you."

"Damn. What's his number?"

I give him Warren's number and remind him to just be cool and tell Warren straight-up if he wants to know details about his convictions.

I'm smiling when I hang up with Petey, and I don't know why. I understand Warren can't guarantee him anything, but just knowing he's willing to at least talk to my brother makes me feel good.

I know Petey's got it in him to be great, and I really wish he'd straighten up for Dana's sake. It's bad enough the child has a dysfunctional mother, too. Petey didn't even know he was a father until Dana was seven years old. I just happened to be on the phone with Mama that day when the woman showed up to Mama's front door. Mama said she opened the door and the woman was standing there with Dana, holding one small suitcase and a giant stuffed rabbit. She pushed Dana towards Mama and said, "Tell your son it's his turn now. I got a lot going on."

A few months after that was when Petey went to prison. So he's never really had the chance to bond with Dana. In one of the letters he wrote to Mama while in the pen he asked if he should get a DNA test. She told him that wouldn't be necessary. Mama said she took one look at Dana when she opened the front door and knew she was ours.

* * *

Ms. Yolanda runs a hand through my hair then pops me on the shoulder with her metal-tooth comb. “You ain’t been here in almost three months,” she says, turning me around to face the mirror. “Look at these ends.”

It’s as if I’ve stuck my hand in an electrical socket, the current choosing my hair as the exit. My ’fro looks a frayed mess under these bright lights. “I’m sorry, Ms. Yolanda,” I say, dodging her eyes. “I’ve been so busy these last couple of months. With closing on my house… moving… work as usual. Y’know….”

“Uhn-huh,” she says on a laugh, and gives me a playful nudge in the back of the head anyway. “That’s no excuse to neglect your head, child.”

Mama started bringing me and Tan to Ms. Yolanda when we were kids, and she’s like an auntie to us. She’s the best stylist in Kashmere Gardens as far as I’m concerned, so no matter how far across the city I move, I will always make the drive back to my hood every two weeks for hair care.

She wraps the cape around me and grabs her scissors. “What you thinking about today? You wanna iron it out? You haven’t done that in a while.”

“Not today. I’m thinking twists… so I don’t have to do too much maintenance.”

“Coming right up,” she says.

Three hours later I leave the salon with my hair well-conditioned and oiled and smelling like a field of spring flowers.

I stop by Target again because it came to mind as I sat under Ms. Yolanda’s hair dryer I forgot to buy cotton balls earlier.

I go in for cotton balls only, but come out with another swimsuit (adding to the two I bought at the mall), a pair of sunglasses, an umbrella just because it was too cute to leave on the rack, and a straw tote bag.

Excitement is coursing through my veins now. In just a few hours I will be on my way to four days of relaxation. The workday went by without incident, and it made me proud when Carmen called to tell me not to worry about anything going on at the office. "Go enjoy your vacation," she said. "I got this."

* * *

Give me a call when you get back in town...

I'm lying in bed right now. Thinking about the cruise and Warren at the same time. What would it be like to have him on the cruise with me? Lounging on deck while we sip margaritas, the ocean breeze blowing through our hair? Well, my hair, his bald head.

I would love to know what that wide back looks like without clothing. Maybe he can be the remedy to this drought of mine.

I'm browsing images of the cruise ship online and my screen starts flashing with an incoming call from Tan.

"No fucking way." I put the phone down on the pillow next to me and turn over on my side so I can get some sleep.

It continues to vibrate, the flash lighting up the room like the police.

The vibrating finally stops seconds later, so I close my eyes.

I force myself to imagine turquoise blue water, white sand between my toes. No emails. No phone calls. Nobody needing anything from me.

But I wish I didn't care so much. Five minutes later it vibrates again, so I find myself grudgingly pressing the button to answer my sister.

"I did it, sis," she says. "I'm done."

"What're you talking about, Tan?"

"I left him."

"You left?"

"Yeah. Me and the girls."

"Why? What happened?"

"I just can't do it no more," she says, her usual refrain. "I left everything there with him. Me and the girls just took our clothes and bed linen, and they toys and computers."

"Tan, you're not making any sense. Where are you now?"

"We at the store right now. I let them go inside to get some snacks."

"So your car is fixed?"

"No. Sookie let me use her daddy's truck since he don't hardly drive no more. So... I'm calling to see if you'll let us come and stay with you for a couple weeks until I can find us an apartment."

I sit up in bed, my mind going a mile a minute. "Tan! Tan! Are you serious?"

"I told you, Millie. I was serious."

I can't believe what I'm hearing. I'm actually beginning to sweat right now I'm so fired up. I throw back the covers and swing my legs over the side of the bed. "Tan, I haven't even been in my house for a full two months. I don't have everything set up or decorated how I want it yet. Where are the girls gonna sleep? Why would you leave without a plan?"

"I couldn't spend another day in that house with him."

"Okay, sis, but this isn't the way to do this! You didn't think this through!"

"It's just until I can find an apartment, Millie," she says quietly, as if I'm the one being ridiculous right now.

I know five minutes have gone by as I sit here, looking

to the ceiling, shaking my head, searching for some sort of sign that this is a bad dream.

“I’m sorry, sis,” I hear myself saying, “but I got a lot going on—”

4

setting sail

"Hey, Mama. Just calling to let you know I'm leaving."

"Where the hell you going?"

"Vacation. I'm on Forty-five right now, headed to Galveston to catch the ship."

"Catch the ship? *What ship?*"

"I'm going on a cruise, Mama."

"What the hell you mean you going on a cruise, Millicent? And why you just now telling me? Hell, I wanna go on a cruise!"

I laugh. "I wanted it to be a surprise."

"How is it a surprise? It ain't like you taking me with you. Who you going with?"

"No one."

"When you coming back?"

"Monday."

"I'll be damned. Hell, I wanna take a cruise, too. Shit."

"Maybe you can go with me next time."

"Mm."

"Did Tan call you?"

"No. Why?"

"She said she left Darell, and she wants to come and stay with me until she can find a place—"

"That damn girl don't know what the hell she wants to do."

"I think she's serious this time, Mama. She called me last night."

"Chile, I ain't studyin' Tan. She ain't leaving Darell. Now, where you say you cruising to?"

"It's just a four-day cruise to Cozumel Mexico."

"You ain't scared are you?"

"Scared of what?"

"Hell, I don't know. It seems fun and scary at the same time. All that water. You got you a bathing suit to wear? Shit… I sho' wanna go. Damn. I hate you even called me." She laughs. "Next time you decide to go on vacation without me, don't even call and let me know."

"I had to call, Mama, so you would know where I am in case anything happens."

"Mm."

"I feel bad though, Ma."

"About what?"

"Tan. I couldn't even sleep last night."

"We been dealing with Tan and Darell since they was thirteen years old. They ain't going nowhere."

"But she said she took the girls. All they had with them were their clothes and toys. They were in the parking lot of some store, and I told her she couldn't come and stay with me. What if they slept in the parking lot somewhere, Ma?"

"Tan crazy, but she ain't *that* crazy. She would've took her ass back home to Darell and slept in the garage before she had them girls sleeping out on the streets."

A deep sigh escapes me. "I don't know…."

"Millie, don't worry about Tan. I'll call her and find out what's going on. You better enjoy yourself on that ship."

I park my SUV in the terminal's parking garage. With my suitcase trailing behind me I cross the street to the ship.

This boat is massive! Good lord, what am I getting myself into? This is my first time cruising. I look around at all the other travelers with their suitcases. They're already in their sun hats and flip flops and they're talking excitedly about the fun to come. I have no idea where I'm supposed to go, so I just fall in line behind them.

A gentleman wearing a Hawaiian print shirt and khaki pants approaches me. "Good day, Miss. Would you like me to take your bag?"

Now, I've heard about scammers taking advantage of travelers, so for a second I am unsure. *How do I know you work here, mister? And where are you taking my bag?* Instead, I glance around me to see what the other people are doing, and I see they're handing off their luggage, so I guess it's okay.

I smile and say, "Of course. Thank you." Then I reach in my purse to give him a tip.

The line of passengers snakes around inside the terminal. I remember reading on the website this ship holds about four thousand people.

I've got my passport and my birth certificate and I wait in line with the others to go through the security check. Couples and families chat with each other, and I suddenly think about what Kya said about being lonely. There is no one in line for me to talk to. No one to make plans with for what we would like to do first.

The thought doesn't last for long though. This is my time.

"Step this way, please."

After a good thirty minutes in line, I finally make it through security, and now I'm being beckoned for a photo op.

I stand in front of a cruise ship backdrop to have my picture taken. I turn to my best side, lay my hands on my hips, and throw my head back with my mouth wide open in faux laughter.

"That's the spirit," the photographer says as he snaps the photo, and I hear several chuckles in line behind me.

Then there's more walking. If I had to guess I'd say I've walked a full two miles already and we haven't even made it inside the ship yet.

We finally cross a threshold from the tunnel and three uniformed officials are standing there waiting to greet us. I assume it's the captain, the co-captain, but I don't know what the lady's title would be. The captain is dressed in a crisp white uniform. He's handsome.

"Welcome," he says in a heavy accent. Is he Italian? Russian?

The photos I saw online don't do this ship justice. "Whoa," I say as soon as I step into the corridor. It's like being inside of a multi-story shopping mall. A fancy shopping mall with dark wood walls and chrome accents. A huge winding staircase leads up to somewhere, but instead of being able to climb that staircase, we are corralled like cattle and led further down the hall to a bank of elevators that will take us to the upper deck.

Once off the elevator we step through automatic doors and there's a party already going on. Music is blasting and people are dancing. Line dancing to the Cha-Cha slide. What's interesting is the cruise ship staff is leading the dance! Did they learn this during job training?

I'm grinning in amazement watching all these bodies, young and old, cha-chaing in all seriousness. I stand here for a few minutes, my hips and shoulders swaying, and I'm tempted to fall right in line with them, but I don't. Instead I look around to see what else is going on. I look above where we are and see the colorful jumbo water slide. Might as well be a kid again. I make a mental note to take a slide at least one time before the cruise ends. Hundreds of white lounge chairs lay out around us and on the decks above. There's a small pool to the left of the make-shift dance floor.

I step away from the party and go in search of food. A long line is outside of this one bar, so I'm guessing their food is good. I step towards the front to peek over a couple of shoulders and see they're serving burgers. I don't have the taste for a burger this early, so I go inside to see what else is offered.

And there is plenty to choose from. There's a deli section serving all types of meat and cheeses, a lot of which I don't even recognize. There're soups and a salad bar. A stir-fry station. I decide to stand in line for an omelet.

Once I have my omelet, I go back to the salad bar for some fresh fruit, and then take a seat at a table right next to the window.

I check the time on my watch. The ship doesn't leave until 4 p.m. What should I do for the next two hours? I wasn't sure what to expect since this is my first cruise, so when I received notice boarding time starts at twelve noon, I left my house early enough to make sure I would be one of the first to board. I guess everyone else had the same idea, considering how long the check-in line was.

So I've just been sitting here staring out of the window, looking at the gray Gulf water. I wonder how far out we have to be before it turns blue? Others around me are dining and chatting quietly. Maybe I can go back out to the deck and watch the line dancers.

I take the remaining slice of honeydew from my plate. The melon is so sweet and tender I should get up and get some more, but I don't want anybody to snatch my table.

I've realized in the short time I've been onboard these window seats are a hot commodity.

I'm tempted to call Mama again and find out if she's talked to Tan, but Mama can go on and on sometimes. Plus, this trip is supposed to be about total relaxation. Especially of the mind. Definitely no phones.

I grab my little red tumbler for a drink of lemonade. I chose to not buy the soda card once I found out there's unlimited lemonade available. Besides, I can hurt myself with some Diet Coke. And like most of the DC drinkers I know proclaim, it's not about the diet part, it's about the taste.

A family of five comes and sits two tables over from me. They look so wholesome and sweet in their coordinating outfits of navy, white, and khaki. The father is tall and lean, wearing navy trouser shorts, which hit him just above the knees; a short-sleeved seersucker shirt, and tan deck shoes with no socks. Mom is also dressed in trouser shorts (khaki), a white eyelet blouse. Her hair is a thick ponytail down her back. Sunglasses perched atop her head. She's carrying a baby who looks to be maybe nine or ten months old in a carrier across her chest. The baby grins and kicks playfully, trying to get her big brother and sister's attention. The little boy has the same black curly hair as his father, and is also dressed in navy and white. The sister has on a khaki jumper, white socks with ruffles, and white Keds tennis shoes. Her hair is two thick pom-poms hanging halfway down her arms.

The baby has only a patch of curls in the front of her little head, so judging by the rest of the family, a luxuriously thick mane is definitely in her future.

The mom and dad speak softly to one another for a few minutes before he walks away, while the children are engrossed in their books. The girl is reading Jacqueline

Woodson. I recognize the cover because it was on Dana's reading list one summer.

It's a beautiful sight to see. Young readers.

Mom catches me staring, so I quickly say, "I was just admiring how focused they are. I can't believe they're reading with all of this going on around them."

She smiles back and says, "Yeah. It's their happy place."

The dad returns shortly with a tray of sandwiches for everybody. Mom reaches in a bag and passes out wipes. They hold hands, pray, and then they eat.

I've never really thought seriously about whether or not I want a family. I know for a lot of women they have it all planned out: married by 25, first baby at 27, another one by 30. When I was with my ex I didn't try to *not* have a baby. Because I certainly wasn't on any type of birth control. And this was before he'd even proposed. I figured we were together, he said he'd found what he was looking for, so it didn't matter what happened.

Thank God I didn't end up pregnant since we didn't last.

There was no major incident that made me call off the engagement. There was no big argument, no cheating. Nothing like that. I just had to get honest with myself and admit there was no chemistry.

When I think about my husband, the man I am to spend the rest of my life with, I think about one who sets my soul on fire when he walks into the room. One I can't keep my hands off of. With my ex, the sparks were never there, but I stayed for four years because I believed I could learn to love him. Some say you shouldn't marry for love anyway, but I don't understand that point of view. I definitely don't need a man for his resources. I can take care of myself.

By the second year of our relationship he'd become a serious gamer. Initially I had no issues with it, figured at least he was home and not out in the streets doing crazy things like spending money gambling or entertaining other women. But it got to the point where he was consumed by the game. He would be on his phone gaming while using the bathroom. He'd eat his dinner in front of the TV, playing the game while I dined alone at the dinner table. The first thing he'd do on the weekends was take a piss and then sit on the living room sofa to game all day. Many times this was before he'd even washed his face and brushed his teeth. He neglected yard work and other chores because of it.

I began to nag and complain about him always being on the game. One night he told me straight-up, 'Quit being a bitch! I don't say anything about your HGTV obsession…' I had to laugh because he was comparing apples to oranges. HGTV does not consume hours and hours of my time, and I only watched it to gain tips on how to add value to our home—correction… *his home*—since he was always talking about doing renovations.

Our incompatibility and lack of chemistry was my reasoning to end the engagement.

* * *

Finally.

I grab my tote bag and leave the table once the announcement is made over the intercom my floor is ready, that we can go to our cabins.

I'm on deck 6. A tip from online cruise reviewers suggested it's a good idea to get a room in the middle of the ship (vertically and horizontally if you can) so you don't feel so much motion from the ocean.

The hallway is long and narrow. One can run from one

end to the next in a straight shot.

Our luggage is waiting for us outside our cabins. I guess the cruise line has faith in its passengers and trusts no one would dare steal somebody else's belongings.

I slide the key into the slot and open the door. It's so warm and cozy-looking! Just like in the photo. White bed linens with a peach-colored blanket draped neatly over the foot of the bed. Sitting on top of the blanket is a towel folded into the shape of a swan. So cute.

I notice the demarcation down the center of the bed, which lets me know it's two twin beds pushed together to form a queen. I walk over to look out of the window. I wanted a room with a balcony, but decided it was much more than I desired to spend. It's bad enough I had to pay the two-person occupancy price. Besides, a lot of the reviews I read mentioned how little time you are actually in your room, so a balcony is only necessary if you plan to spend a lot of time out there.

The bathroom is small, but it's clean. I unpack my luggage, hanging my sundresses and wraps in the closet; shorts and tops go in the drawers. Then I lay out my toiletries in the bathroom. There's a safe, so I lock my passport and birth certificate inside since I won't need them anymore.

I take a seat on the bed when I'm done. We're provided a printed schedule for the day's activities. There's bingo. Trivia games. A casino. A cigar bar. Spa.

Hmm... a massage sounds nice.

Another call comes over the intercom. We have to come down for the safety briefing. I've gotten good about following the crowd, because I sure as heck don't know where to go, and the ship map is a little confusing.

There are so many people lined up shoulder-to-shoulder once I make it to my assigned area.

Is this really every single person that's aboard the ship? Are we all literally standing on one side of this ship? Will it start leaning? I know I'm being paranoid right now and thinking foolishly.

I wish people would stop talking so we can actually hear the instructions. I can't stand it when people are rude. I'm pretty sure if something happens—God forbid—and this ship starts to go down, the ones yapping their mouths right now will be the first ones hollering like fools because they won't know what to do.

The lady behind me is talking about how this is her fifteenth cruise, and I'm so tempted to turn around and tell her to shut up, to show some consideration for those of us who actually care about our safety.

* * *

The briefing went quickly. We were informed that our safety vests and the same instructions we received can be found in our cabin closets.

Should I freshen up and change clothes? I signed up for early dining, so my dinner is not until six o'clock. I heard the dinners can be quite elegant, three- and four-course meals. I wonder what they're serving us.

My phone rings as I consider this. I'm tempted to let it go to voicemail, wanting to adhere to my no phones rule, when I see it's neither Mama nor Carmen. But what if it's Tan calling from another number because her phone is dead after spending a night in the truck?

"Hello?"

"Millicent?"

"Warren?" I'm sure I saved his number in my phone, but his name didn't show on my screen.

"How you doing? Are you having fun?"

Smiling, I say, “I’m still here in Galveston. The ship hasn’t left yet.”

“Oh? I thought you would’ve been halfway there by now.”

“No. Not yet.” I laugh shortly. “We sail at four.”

“I just had to talk to you again,” he says. “Tell you I’m jealous. I wish I were going with you.”

“Do you really?” I don’t know what else to say because I surely can’t tell him I’ve already imagined him here with me in the most scandalous of ways.

“It would’ve been great for us to experience our first cruise together.”

Our first cruise? Why do I feel light-headed all of a sudden? “Well... I’m not sure how your wife would feel about that....”

“My wife?”

“Your girlfriend then?”

He chuckles. “I have neither,” he says.

So my fantasies are definitely *warranted.* Mm. “Did Petey call you?” I ask before my mind veers off into a world of hot cabin nights with sweaty sheets.

“No. He didn’t.”

“*What?*”

“That’s another thing I wanted to tell you,” Warren says. “Did you tell him to call me yesterday?”

“Of course I did, and he told me he would.”

“Hunh. Well, I never received a call from him,” Warren says.

I am pissed. What the heck happened to Petey? “I am so sorry, Warren,” I say. “Maybe he copied your number down wrong when I gave it to him, because I can’t think of a reason why he wouldn’t call. He was excited when I told him about the position.” My level of pisstivity just went up twenty degrees because I have to make up a scenario just to cover his ass even though I know Petey had the correct number because he repeated it back to me.

"No problem. Just have him call my business line. This number I'm calling you from is my personal cell. I want you to have it."

I smile despite my embarrassment. "Okay. I will. Thank you."

"Have a good time," he says, and we hang up.

Are we moving? We must be moving. I go over to the window. Yes, we are finally pulling away from the dock! I want to see this live and in person, not behind this square window.

Grabbing my tote bag, I hurry out of the room for the nearest deck.

Everyone else has the same idea because I can barely find a space to stand next to the railing. I decide to go up a deck, and take the stairs.

Ahhh... yes. Finally setting sail.

I stand here, watching as we move slowly away from the port. It feels kind of funny beneath my feet, the tug as we push through the water.

Four days of relaxation has begun.

I reach into my tote for my phone. But first I must call Petey to find out what his fucking problem is.

5

a day at sea

Stretching languidly across the bed, my eyes flutter open, a moan of ecstasy escapes me. What a wonderful night of sleep. I don't remember dreaming about anything, it was so good.

The gentle rocking of the boat convinces me to stay here a little bit longer, so I reach over for the remote to turn on the TV. There is a channel that shows live footage of the Lido deck, so you can see what is going on outdoors from the comfort of your cabin. I discovered the channel last night while in bed. At one point I saw a young boy dart across the screen; seconds later, a girl came chasing after him. I laughed and shook my head, thinking about the parents who were probably tucked away in their rooms and assumed their children were too, since it was after midnight, but had no idea their kid was out running amok.

An hour passes, and my bladder can no longer stand the pressure, so I go ahead and get up.

Pulling back the curtains, my eyes widen in amazement. Nothing but deep blue sea to the left, right, and front of me. We are literally floating on the ocean! I wonder what type of life is out there. Will I see dolphins leaping out of the water? A whale's sprout? Or do the creatures feel the vibration of this gigantic vessel from miles away and get the hell out of dodge?

One thing I noticed is that, while we cruise during daytime hours, this ship converts to a speed boat after dark. It was during dinner last night when I realized how fast we were traveling. I looked out of our dining room window to see waves of white foam as we jetted through the water.

The dinner was awkward to say the least. My assigned seat was at a big round table with seven other cruisers. There was a married couple and their two teenage children, another husband and wife, the wife's sister, and then there was me. We began with the basics: where in Texas we're from, whether or not this was our first cruise, and which activities we planned to partake in following dinner.

I'm not sure what I was thinking when I signed up for my dinner plan. I assumed I would be seated by myself since I was traveling by myself. It would have been a much better experience to have my own table where I could dine in peace and not subject myself to bland conversations and forced laughter.

I will check with Guest Services later to find out if I can change my seating arrangement.

I go to the closet to decide what to wear. It's a day at sea, and I know now it can get windy and chilly on deck, so I decide on a pair of leggings and flowy tunic. Back in the bathroom, I pull off my silk bonnet, run my fingers through my twists to fluff them out.

Island music is playing as I step through the double doors leading to the Lido deck. There are even more people out here now. It's so surreal to see us on this big boat in the middle of this massive sea.

The line for the burger grill is twice as long today. I bypass it again and go inside. Yesterday's omelet was delicious, but I don't want to limit myself. I plan to partake in a little of everything. And today there are too many choices. The stir fry station is busy too. I stand in the buffet line and choose some breakfast sausage. There's a waffle oven, so I go there next to make a Belgian waffle.

I sit and people watch for a bit and read the activity schedule. Let's see... I think I will go and browse the shops, and then make it to the main lobby for the twelve o'clock trivia game.

For the most part, everybody I've seen is with someone. I don't recall anyone walking around by themselves. And if they are, it's because they're making their way back to be near their wife/husband/partner/traveling companion. Only a brave soul would decide to cruise alone.

I think about Mama and try to imagine what it would be like to have her here. Knowing her, she probably would abandon me, going off to do her own thing. The casino and cigar bar would be her favorite hangouts, I know. And the pool.

Only a miracle could get Tan on a cruise. The main reason being because she can't afford room and board for six people. Throughout their marriage, she and Darell have always done little things with the girls. My sister loves to pack a lunch for her family and drive them to Deussen Park where they can sit by the lake while the girls run and play. Or they go to Kemah and spend a day on the boardwalk. One time they drove to San Antonio to visit SeaWorld. But, as far as a real, overnight-stay-in-a-nice-hotel-type of vacation, my sister has never had the experience. And she's never been outside of Texas.

Swallowing down my milk, I try not to think about it, but it's hard. Last night, right before I fell asleep, I called

Mama. I needed an excuse to try out the Wi-Fi package I'd bought. She said she finally got in touch with Tan, that my sister sounded tired, but wouldn't tell her where she and the girls were. I tossed all night, thinking... what type of auntie am I? My sister reaches out for my help, and I close the door on her. What if she's gone to a shelter? I'm hoping she's with a friend. She has plenty of them. But how is that a safe and comfortable place for my nieces? How sad is it they have to stay with strangers when their auntie has a whole spare room and living room where they can lay their heads? A place with no distractions where they can study and do their homework?

* * *

I visit the clothing and accessories shop first. My souvenirs budget quickly goes out of the window after seeing all the cute stuff they have. I end up buying five tote bags and fill them with all types of cruise memorabilia for my nieces: water bottles, T-shirts, flip flops, hats, ink pens, water globes, inflatable beach balls for the littlest ones. Mama and Tan get sarongs, key chains, and matching beach towels.

My frustration with Petey should dissuade me from spending a dime on him, but I buy his trifling behind a T-shirt, cap, and wine bottle opener anyway.

Yesterday he told me he decided not to give Warren a call when he realized he wouldn't have transportation to get to wherever the potential job site might be, that the Metro bus line didn't travel to The Woodlands. He is right, and I for damn sure didn't consider that fact, but I cussed his ass out anyway and told him to call and find out the specifics first before he made any rash decisions. I will figure out a way to get him to and from work if he makes it through the hiring process.

Once I have all the gifts for my family, and my triple-digit purchase receipt, I leave the store and cross the hall for the jewelry shop.

Beautiful, shiny watches, necklaces, and rings line the cases. They even have wedding bands. I wonder how many men proposed to their girlfriend while out on a cruise. I've come across a few handsome men onboard, but they were with someone of course. Only a clueless individual would think they could meet a single person on a cruise. Well, anything is possible, but what are the odds?

"See something you would like to try?"

The saleslady is smiling at me, a woman who's not much taller than the case itself.

"Twenty percent off sale today," she says. "You should buy now before it is gone. Which one you like?"

This makes me chuckle. "Umm—"

"Which one?" she says, removing the coil keychain from her wrist, ready to unlock the case.

My intentions were to come in and see what type of jewelry they have, not to actually buy anything since I've already spent enough money for today. But the charms catch my eye. Mama bought me and Tan charm bracelets for our twentieth birthdays, and I've slowly added to mine over the years.

I point at a cruise ship charm. It will be a great way to commemorate my first cruise. "Let me see that one, please."

"Yes, sure."

Once I have it in my hand, I decide to buy the flat versus the 3D one instead. "And I'll take the sun charm, too," I tell the saleslady. "For my sister."

The lobby is full once I make it down for the trivia game, and a kind gentleman insists I take his chair while he sits on the floor next to his wife's chair. I didn't have time to drop my bags off at my cabin, so I have them all sitting on the floor at my feet.

I'm given a piece of paper the size of an index card and a miniature pencil to write with. On the paper are fifteen numbered lines.

"Okay..." the trivia host begins. "This is how the game goes.... I'm going to play five seconds of a song. You have to guess the song's title. Bonus point if you can name the artist. *Do not* blurt out the answer, simply write it on your answer sheet. We have a prize for the one who gets the most right."

We're all giddy, pencils poised over our paper.

The first song is played, and immediately there are gasps of excitement as people recognize the song. I don't have a clue what it is. But that's okay, I've got fourteen more tries.

Songs two, three, and four are played and my answer sheet is still blank. I should get up and take my ass back to my cabin because they ain't playing shit I know, but I stay put because it will be too much of a distraction trying to gather all these bags and make an exit.

When the thumping bassline of the next song comes in, my heart flutters. I know this one! Other cruisers are rocking and clapping their hands because they know the song too.

I go to write down my answer and realize I don't actually know the title of the song. Dangit! I know this song. I swear I do.

The host has cut the sample, but the music's still going in my head.

Hey! Hey! And another one gone... And another one gone.

Another one bites the dust!

That's it! I quickly write down my answer because they've moved on to song six. I try to think of the artist's name to earn an extra point so I'll have at least two, but my mind draws a total blank. Dammit!

Song thirteen is the only other one I recognize. Marvin Gaye's *Let's Get It On.*

Once the game is over, the host plays the list again, calling out the answers.

"How'd you do?" the husband beside me asks.

I shake my head. "A measly two out of fifteen."

His wife laughs. "We didn't do much better. Only five right."

"We're more into country," he adds.

"Yeah?" I nod. "I didn't know any of these songs. But it was fun." I gather my bags and stand to leave. "Thanks again for the seat. Enjoy the rest of the cruise."

"You, too," they say.

* * *

I've found a quiet corner in the rear of the ship. There's very little traffic back here, so I stretch out in one of the lounge chairs. I have my laptop with me, and even though I said I wouldn't, I can't help logging in to check my emails.

I'm surprised I haven't received a phone call from the office. Not that I'm wishing for one, either. I can't remember a time I've taken a vacation where I was able to truly relax without being bothered. Something always came up: a resident wanted to complain about an event; a rec aid needed to report an incident that occurred during summer camp; a caterer botched our order and we ran out of food for a ceremony.

"Are there power outlets over here?"

A sister wearing the exact same dress I wanted from Nordstrom approaches carrying a laptop.

"I'm not sure," I say, and sit up to scan the walls behind me, helping her search.

"Oh. I'm sorry," she says. "I thought you were plugged in."

I smile. "No. I told myself I can use the computer for only twenty minutes, then I have to shut it right back down."

"I've got to send off something for work," she tells me.

"You're working while on vacation, too?"

"Yes," she groans.

"Me too. I said I wasn't going to log in, and here I am."

"It's like... you just know it's gonna be hectic when you get back, so you try to stay ahead of it, y'know?"

"Tell me about it. I'm sorry. I'm Millicent. What's your name?"

"Oh my god," she says. "I never thought I'd ever in my life come across another person with that name."

"Is your n—"

"I have a cousin named Millicent." She laughs. "I'm Cherise."

"Oh, okay. My grandmother is the only person I know with the name," I say.

"Well... I guess I have to go inside to find an outlet. My friend is already upset with me, claiming I'm a workaholic. If she sees me with this laptop, she'd probably take it and toss it overboard."

"Oh no!" I laugh.

"It was nice meeting you, Millicent."

"You too, Cherise."

"Don't work too hard now," she says over her shoulder as she walks away.

"I won't," I say. But as soon as I log into my email, I see

one from the superintendent. She's tried to phone me several times, and I need to call the office.

* * *

Daaang!

What *doesn't* this cruise ship have?

I'm sitting here, waiting for the show to start. If I didn't know I was on a boat, I would say I was in a fancy New York theater, about to witness a Broadway musical. Cruisers are piling in, claiming a spot in the plush seating.

Here I go again, worrying about whether the ship can withstand so many bodies on one end.

"Millicent!"

Oh god. Please don't tell me somebody I know is here.

I look to my left, trying to see who's calling my name.

"Millicent! Up here," they say, and I spot an arm waving frantically on the balcony above.

I don't recognize the woman, but then I see Cherise sitting next to her. Cherise waves and mouths for me to come up and sit with them. I'm reluctant to go because I have a perfect view: main floor, center-stage.

"Are you leaving?" the old lady next to me asks as I stand.

A *yes* is only half-way out of my mouth before she slaps her heavy purse onto the seat.

"Just so you know," Cherise says when I finally make it to them, "I was only pointing you out to my friend. She's the one who decided to call you out in front of everybody."

"That's because she was too coward to do it herself. I'm not worried about people looking at me like I'm crazy. I told her, 'How else were you gonna hear me in a room with two-hundred other people?'" She extends an arched hand my way. "Eve McKinney," she says in a professional tone."

"Millicent Green," I return with the same intense professionalism.

Cherise rolls her eyes, shaking her head. Me and Eve laugh, and then we take our seats to get ready for the show.

"That was a-ma-zing," Eve says when it's over, and everyone else is in agreement because the entire room is standing in ovation.

"It really was," Cherise nods.

"Those dancers! Geez... makes me wanna join a dance troupe," I say.

"The singers, the costumes, everything was perfect."

"I think they have another show." Cherise pulls out her activity schedule. "Do y'all wanna stay for that one?"

The man seated in the row behind us lets us know it will be the same performance, just shown at a later time.

"Okay... and?" Eve says after he leaves his row. "Maybe we *want* to see the same performance. Thank-you-very-much, Mr. Eavesdropper."

"Girl, stop," Cherise tells her friend. "He's just being nice."

"But nobody's talking to him."

I laugh quietly. I'm guessing Eve is a firecracker. Picking up my bag from the floor, I say, "Well, ladies... thanks for inviting me up. Maybe I'll see y'all around again."

"What're you about to do now?" Cherise asks. "We're gonna go to our room and change into our bathing suits. Hang out at the pool for a bit. You can come with us if you want to."

"Maybe even hit the club," Eve adds.

"There's a club?" I say.

"You mean you didn't know?" She snakes her body, snapping her fingers. "We were in that thang last night. Cuttin' up!"

"It was nice," Cherise says. "The deejay played a good mix."

I had planned on turning in for the night, to go to my cabin, shower, and watch television until I fell asleep. But I guess I can hang out for another two or three hours.

And these sisters seem like a lot of fun.

"Where do I meet you? And what time?"

6

cozumel

I feel the consequences of what went down last night all in my legs as soon as my feet hit the floor. Like an old woman with arthritic knees, I limp to the bathroom. Even squatting over the toilet is a challenge, and I bust out laughing at the craziness of it all.

We danced the night away.

Literally.

I have never met someone with as much energy as Eve showed last night. She is the type of woman society would label a BBW, but that voluptuous body put mine and Cherise's to shame because we could barely keep up with her. The woman had us on the dance floor for a full three hours straight! And if we tried to slink away, desperately in need of a break off our heels, she'd pull us right back.

The last time I partied this hard was at Tan and Darell's ten-year wedding anniversary celebration. Much like having a hangover, I feel like my body needs a day to recuperate.

The cabin phone rings as soon as I've washed my hands, so I hurry as fast as my dead legs will allow me to go and answer it.

"Millicent! Where are you? I thought you said you were gonna meet us for breakfast this morning?"

"*What?*" I look at my cell phone for the time. Damn. I overslept. "Y'all are already up?"

"Yeah," Eve says. "We just finished eating. We figured you changed your mind."

"Geez! I had no idea how late it was. I forgot to set my alarm. I'm sorry."

Eve laughs. "No problem. But we're dressed, full, and ready to hit the beach!"

I laugh. "Let me go ahead and get my stuff together and I'll be right down."

We are finally on land, and today is the day we get to leave the ship. If I remember correctly, we're allowed seven or eight hours to explore the port.

"Look at you! Looking all cute. I love that wrap."

"Thank you, girl. You're looking good, too," I return the compliments to Eve. She's wearing a bright orange high waisted two-piece swimsuit underneath a black crochet sheer cover up. Cherise is just as sassy in her green snake-print halter suit with matching robe.

As soon as we step off the ship the photographer asks us to pause for a photo.

The weather is perfect. Blue, cloudless sky. The sun is warm and there's a light breeze that comes through every few minutes, whirling through our cover ups.

As we amble along the pier, I regret spending so much money in the cruise ship's gift shop because there's a lot more here I want to buy. Mexican blankets and dresses. Mugs and trinkets. Art.

Eve rushes over to a cart of velvet sombreros. "We definitely gotta get us one! You can't go to Mexico without buying a sombrero!"

I pick up a navy blue one with silver accents. Cherise grabs a black one, and Eve chooses red. The three of us try them on, and following Eve's lead, me and Cherise set one leg out and bow into a shoulder shimmy.

The vendor grins at our silliness.

We pay for our hats and then leave for the taxi cab station.

It's a short ride to Paradise Beach. Our driver, Miguel, can't stop staring at Eve through the rearview mirror. She and Cherise are in the backseat, while I have the front next to him.

"I am sorry," he says to her. "You make me think of my wife."

"So... what you saying, Miguel? You like 'em thick and chocolate?"

"Yes. Yes, I do." Miguel smiles and me and Cherise giggle like school girls.

"Alright now! Don't you say nothing that's gonna get you in trouble." Eve smacks her thigh, laughing boisterously.

"Ohhh... it's okay. My wife is not here anymore. She pass away."

"I'm sorry to hear that." The three of us seemed to reply at the same time.

"It's okay. It's okay." Miguel nods.

"What happened to her? If you don't mind me asking," Eve says.

"She had a ana-riz... anariz— How you say?"

"Aneurysm?" Cherise helps him out.

"Yes. In the brain."

"Aww." The three of us again.

"I'm sorry."

"We met in Vegas," he tells us. "I was working there at the time. She was a dancer. Cirque du Soleil. Do you know what it is?"

"Uhn-huh," we say.

"She ride in my cab. She didn't drive you see. For a whole

year I chased after her. Long story short… we married on her birthday. Fifteen months after that she was gone."

I'm sure Eve and Cherise feel it right in the chest as I do. My heart aches for him.

"She was so beautiful," Miguel continues, "and I pray every day maybe she come back to me. So when I see you…" He glances at the rearview mirror again. "It make me wonder…"

"Give me another one."

I reach into my tote bag again for the travel pack of Kleenex. Me and Cherise are misty-eyed, but Eve has literal tears skipping down her cheeks.

"I did *not* need to hear that right now," Eve says. She laughs weakly.

"Right. Just… sad." I take a deep breath, dabbing at the corners of my eyes.

"I'm curious to know what her name is," Cherise says. "I'd like to look her up and see some of her shows."

"I can't imagine going through something like that… meeting the person of my dreams only to lose them within a short period of time."

We are lounging in hammocks, shaded underneath a cabana on Paradise Beach. Soft sand stretches for miles along the green-blue water. Eve and Cherise are stuffed from breakfast, and gone quiet. My stomach is growling now, but I'm too lazy to get up and go search for food. The cool breeze, the sound of the waves rushing ashore a few feet away is so relaxing. The fruit and nut mix in my bag will have to do.

As we lay in silence, my mind drifts to the email from the superintendent. She said I'd exceeded the planned budget for the Daddy Daughter event and needed to find a way to cut costs. She was expecting the adjustments be emailed to her by the end of today.

I forwarded the message to Carmen instead, along with some instructions on how to handle it.

I'm no longer going out my way to do something when there are capable people right there in the office who can assist. The last time I checked, the definition for vacation is *rest from work*. So that's what I'm doing from here on out: *resting from work*.

* * *

"Millicent, are you married?"

Cherise had been quiet for so long, I thought she'd fallen asleep. "No," I say. "But I was engaged once."

"Really? What happened?"

Eve lifts her head up from the hammock. "You caught his ass cheating, didn't you?"

Chuckling, I say, "No. It wasn't that." Then I give them the rundown on how I just wasn't that into him. "He would be good for somebody else though," I add. "What about y'all?"

"Divorced," Eve says.

"Married to my job," says Cherise.

"What led to your divorce?" I ask cautiously.

"An affair."

"Oh."

"With our dentist!"

"Are you serious?"

"Yes, girl. For three years we were going to that bitch every six months for cleanings. She all in my face, in my mouth, and I had no idea she was fucking my husband."

I shake my head. "That's crazy."

"Once I found out, I went up to that clinic and dragged her ass all up and down the office by her ponytail."

Gasping, I say, "You didn't!"

Cherise lets out a high-pitched hoot. "She did!"

"Damn. So what happened after that?"

"The staff called the cops; they came and arrested me."

"I bailed her out," Cherise says, still laughing.

"It was the dumbest shit I've ever done," says Eve. "Embarrassing. No man—husband or not—is worth fighting another woman over."

Nodding, I say, "So true."

"I mean... my husband is the one who made those vows to me. The bitch didn't have anything to do with them. I was upset with the wrong person that day."

"What did your husband have to say about it?"

"There was nothing he could say. I didn't give him a chance to. I packed my stuff the same night and never looked back. The divorce papers were served on his job two weeks later."

"Wow. Do y'all have kids together?"

"No. We were part of the 'Married, but Childfree by Choice crowd'."

"I'm sure that made the decision a lot easier."

Eve is quiet for a few minutes, and then she says, "I can see myself doing it again though. I was made to be somebody's wife. My parents have been together for thirty-plus years, so I know how great it can be when you've got the right kind of man."

"What about you, Cherise?" I say.

Eve clucks her tongue. "This girl is so damn frigid, I'm starting to wonder if her ass is asexual."

"That's not true," Cherise counters. "I just don't have much time to do any serious dating. Work keeps me busy."

"What do you do?"

Eve cuts in. "Don't even get her started talking about work. I told her I don't wanna hear one word about her job while we're on this cruise."

"She just wants to know what I do, Eve. Dang."

"You got three seconds," Eve tells her.

"I'm the director of development for a non-profit. I—"

"Ahp! That's it! That's all we need to know."

I laugh along with Cherise.

"This is a vacation," Eve says, and struggles out of the hammock. "C'mon... let's go jump in the ocean."

* * *

"Who would imagine they could get a full-body massage right on the beach?"

I sigh in response, my muscles in full relaxation mode that I'm afraid if I open my mouth drool will spill out.

After an hour of splashing about in the water, we had lunch, and then decided to close out our day in the sun with a soothing massage.

There's a steady breeze now, rustling the sheer white curtains of the cabana, and all I can think about is how this beach is so aptly named.

I try not to cry out in pleasure as the lady who's working on me goes deep into my lower back.

Cherise is quiet on the massage table next to me, and I believe she's really asleep this time. I've been there before—on vacation, but so tired from work and other obligations, that all you want to do is sleep.

"Next time we come," Eve says, "we should go snorkeling."

"You planning on coming here on another cruise?" I say.

"Oh yeah. Might even pay the deposit as soon as we get back on the ship."

I smile and close my eyes again.

Maybe I should do the same.

7

aft

"Miss? Please..."

I look up to see a photographer with the camera aimed at me.

"You are gorgeous," he says, and I give my biggest smile.

The photo is snapped and he disappears as quickly as he came.

That's another thing I noticed while on the cruise. There are photographers all over, roaming the ship, ready to take your photo. The pictures are then developed and waiting for you to purchase at the photo shop.

I make a mental note to go there later tonight to buy this one.

I'm feeling rather cute today. I have on the dress I bought from a shop on the pier when we returned from the beach yesterday: a gold off-the-shoulder Mexican dress, with my jumbo gold hoop earrings. Bored with my twists, I unraveled them, so now I'm rocking my usual twist out. All that is missing is a red flower for my hair.

I'm sitting here in a big, comfy bucket chair next to the window in a quiet section of the ship. That's another thing I realized: just because there are four-thousand people aboard doesn't mean you can't find a place outside of your cabin to escape the noise.

The piano bar is around the corner, so all I hear are the soft notes of someone playing a melody.

Warren floats into mind. I wonder what his bow-legged, sexy ass is doing right now. It is Sunday, so he's probably at home, being a typical man, stretched out on the sofa watching football. I can't wait to see what's to come of our meet-up once I'm back on land. I'm curious to find out more about him, especially why his fine self is single.

"Hey, Millicent! Where've you been?"

Snatched out of my thoughts, I turn away from the window to see this blonde couple standing over me, bearing wide smiles like The Joker.

I blink, trying to place them.

"We haven't seen you at dinner. We've missed you!"

A nervous chuckle comes out as I realize they are the older married couple from our dining room assignment.

"Oh. Um—"

"How are you?" the wife asks.

"We were worried," the husband says, "thinking perhaps you were sick."

Confused, I shake my head. "No. What?"

"I told Steven we shouldn't consider the worst, but couldn't think of a reason why you would skip dinner. They are so special."

"Yeah," Steven agrees. "Last night they served us ginger salmon and roasted asparagus with almonds."

"It was sooo good."

"Ooh! Honey, tell her about the prime rib."

The wife closes her eyes at the memory. "The best we've ever had."

Steven says, "I hear tonight they're gonna have stroganoff with beef tips. I can't wait for that."

Their excitement is so cute! I didn't bother to change my seating arrangement after all. Instead, I opted to eat dinner on the Lido deck for the past couple of nights, which was usually pizza or a chicken tender basket.

"You definitely don't want to miss tonight's dinner," says the wife. "There's gonna be a special performance since this is the last night of the cruise. Will you be there?"

The two of them look at me, bright-eyed with anticipation.

"I can't say for sure because I'm supposed to meet with my friends later."

The wife sighs as if she's really disappointed.

"Ah well. It's unfortunate."

"In case you can't make it, it was nice meeting you, Millicent."

"You too," I say, smiling.

The husband turns and waves at me as they walk away.

I can't put into words the beauty of a sunset while in the middle of the ocean.

Ethereal.

Like we're at the end of the earth.

The golden light shining down gives the water a metallic hue.

For the first time since I've been onboard, I pull out my phone and take a selfie.

I find it interesting that we have not crossed one other ship the entire time we've been at sea. Maybe I assumed we would pass another vessel and wave at the cruisers standing out on their upper decks.

But, no. It's as if we're the only souls out here.

* * *

I admit I am touched that they are genuinely happy to see me return to the table. Who knew they would even care that I wasn't here? Or that they'd remember my name?

It's embarrassing I had to be reminded of their names: Marsha and Steven; their two children—Samantha and Wade. The others are Delana and Jared, and Delana's sister, Christy.

Steven is flattered I've selected the stroganoff from the menu.

Our conversation is friendly and light. Even the teens join in every once in a while.

Christy tells me they saw me at the beach yesterday. They were there, too.

I choose the chocolate lava cake with ice cream for dessert, and just after we are served, the lights go out.

For a second, we all are confused, glancing around the dining room.

The fire alarm sounds, which throws the room into a hushed panic, but then the music starts.

Celebrate good times... come on!

Laughter fills the dining room, and Marsha leans into me. "See... I told you," she says.

Celebrate good times... come on!

The lights pop on again, and we see our servers have put aside their trays and have taken to the aisles and the staircases. All of them are dancing in sync. Before long, the entire dining room is rocking, grooving to the sounds of Kool & the Gang's *Celebration.* Marsha leans into me again, her cell phone in the air as she aims at our table.

She finally gets all of us in frame.

Yahoo!
It's a celebration...

* * *

"Good thing I came in here early to save us a seat."

"You're right. It is packed!" I sit in the half-moon booth next to Eve and Cherise.

It is karaoke night and Eve's secured us a spot in front, right next to the stage.

"I can't remember the last time I've been to a karaoke bar," I say. "I didn't even know it was still a thing."

"I am the karaoke queen," Eve exclaims.

Cherise puts a hand over her mouth and leans towards me. "She put our name down. We're the third act."

"Huh?"

The first act is onstage. A lady singing Adele's *Rolling in the Deep*. Her voice is strong, and it is evident she can sing for real.

"What you mean?" I turn to Cherise.

"We go up after the next one. We're doing 'Push It' by Salt 'n Pepa."

"Oh." I nod. "You mean you and Eve are going up."

Cherise giggles. "No. All three of us."

I chuckle in disbelief, looking over at Eve, but she's clapping, singing along with the lady onstage. "Absolutely not," I say.

"Why not?" She giggles again.

I lean over Cherise, touching Eve's elbow to get her attention. "I know you don't think I'm going up there with y'all."

"C'mon, girl. It'll be fun!"

"No," I say, shaking my head. "Y'all are not about to have me going up there, embarrassing myself."

"Why would you be embarrassed? These people don't

know you. Probably won't see you ever again in life."

"Eve... I'm not."

She only smiles and turns back toward the stage, dancing in her seat.

That's one thing Millicent Green don't do. I would never go up in front of a group of people and perform, making a fool of myself.

Sing and dance in front of an audience? Never!

I don't have a problem dancing. I love to dance. But only in the darkness of a club surrounded by others who are so busy in their own worlds, or under the influence of alcohol, that they don't care how I look. There are about one-hundred and fifty people jammed into this room. No way will I be able to go in front of all these folks and sing and dance without peeing on myself from the nerves.

The second act is on. Poor guy is just standing there, one hand in his pocket, his head down, looking at the teleprompter as he sings some country song.

Eve shakes her head. "See... this is what I don't like. Karaoke is not just about singing the song. You have to perform. You have to entertain..."

When he is done, the crowd emits a sad applause for his effort.

Lord...

Before our name is even called, Eve is out of her seat. Cherise stands up next, and then looks back at me.

"Nope... y'all go 'head."

"Millicent, you too. Come on."

"I'm serious. I'm not doing it," I say.

Eve looks at me.

"I can't."

"Yes you can," she says, her purple lips in a pinch.

Cherise reaches down and grabs my hand, pulling me from the seat.

Oh my god. Oh my god. I am going to faint.

"Eve, seriously," I say as we walk up the short steps to the platform.

"Just follow me and do what I do," she whispers.

She and Cherise take a mic, and suddenly we are onstage, bathed in the bright overhead lights.

Oh god. Oh god. Oh my god.

The intro starts and Eve is saying something to the crowd, but I don't know what, because my mind is a jumbled mess as I look out onto the sea of faces staring back at us.

Psshh... ah-push it!

The beat drops, and Eve takes off. I immediately fall into the groove because there's no turning back now.

Push it good!

Watching Eve, I realize this is definitely not her first time performing this act. She has the routine down to a T, the moves taken straight from the music video.

Cherise is next to her, putting much attitude into her pelvic thrusts.

Push it real good!

I close my eyes for a second, pumping my body, doing my own thing, trying not to appear so awkward looking to Eve for direction. Sweat is pouring down my back, and I know it's the combination of these stage lights and my nerves.

If only Mama and Tan and my nieces were here to witness this, because I know they won't believe me when I tell them about it.

I can't believe it.

Cherise is approaching me with the mic, grinning, when I open my eyes. They want me to take the second verse!

Wide-eyed, I shake my head. *I'll be damned!*

The audience laughs.

Cherise is still dancing, never missed a beat. Eve encourages me from the foreground with a nod.

These heffas are crazy!

I grab the mic and step forward. "Yo yo yo yo, baby-pop... Yeah, you come here, give me a kiss. Better make it fast or else I'm gonna get pissed..."

This is no longer just karaoke. We are in concert. We *are* Salt 'n Pepa.

Eve falls into the famous back-bend. Cherise goes next, and I follow.

The crowd loves us.

It is the longest four-and-a-half minutes of my life.

The song ends, we leave the stage, cruisers are still going crazy, and I swear it feels like I'm on the verge of a heart attack.

* * *

It's taken me a while to calm down. I'm in my room now, fresh from the shower even though I'm headed right back out to the upper deck. I had to get rid of the body sweat. And boy, was I wet! Even my underwear were soaked through.

Cherise suggested we meet at the hot tub in the rear of the ship.

I thought I would be anxious to return home by now, but I'm kinda sad to be honest. I wish we had three more days to cruise. It feels like the real fun is just getting started.

* * *

"Oooh... I like this bathing suit even better than the one you wore yesterday," Eve tells me.

She and Cherise are already in the hot tub.

"Thank you, girl. Found this at Target."

"Oh really?"

"I love Target," Cherise says.

"Yep. So do I," I say. I grabbed this lemon-colored two-piece off the rack as soon as I saw it. I sit my bag next to the tub and step in. "I'm surprised no one else is out here."

"Oh, there were others here," Eve says. "But they got out as soon as we got in."

We laugh.

"Good," I say.

It's quiet for a few minutes. The water feels divine. I stretch out my legs.

"You gotta admit, Millicent... that was fun as hell." Eve laughs.

"I still can't believe I did that!"

"We told you," Cherise says.

"I have never done anything like that in my life."

"I wish it could've been recorded."

"Yeah. That would've been nice to show my sister and my nieces. But, y'all gotta be honest with me.... How many times have y'all performed that song?"

Cherise laughs, looking over at her friend. "This is only my second time, right? Performing it with you?"

"Salt 'n Pepa are my girls," Eve says. "They're my karaoke go-to."

It is quiet again. Eve lays her head back on the edge of the tub.

Cherise says, "How about a game of Truth or Dare?"

"Oh lord," Eve says.

"C'mon... it's our last night on the ship."

"I'm down," I say.

"Alright. Then you can be first. Truth or Dare?"

"Truth."

"Wait a minute," Eve says, raising her head. "It's first to ask a question, right?"

"I don't think it matters, Eve," Cherise says, rolling her eyes playfully. Then she looks at me. "Do you prefer to ask or be asked?"

I shrug. "I don't care, really. Ask away."

"Okay." Cherise clears her throat. "Who is your celebrity crush? Male and female."

"That's easy!"

"Hush!" Cherise tells Eve. "It's not your turn."

"Morris Chestnut," I say.

"That's a good one."

"Mmm-hmm," Eve groans.

"For female? I'd say.... Wait... this is just a female we admire, right? Not somebody we're fantasizing about hooking up with?"

"Yes."

"Although we wouldn't have a problem with it if that's what you fancy," Eve says.

We laugh.

"Oprah. For her money and her impact of course."

They nod in agreement.

"Your turn, Eve."

"Okay. Truth or Dare?"

"Truth," says Cherise.

"Name a celebrity you are ashamed to admit you find sexy or attractive."

"Ooh." Cherise is thoughtful for a second, and then says, "Lil Wayne."

"Lil Wayne?!" Me and Eve are disgusted.

Giggling, Cherise says, "There's something about him. He looks like he needs a hug."

"Lil Wayne?" Eve says again.

"I'm serious."

Eve lays her head back down. "You know what? I'm gonna leave that one alone."

"Truth or Dare?" I say to Eve.

"Truth."

"When was the last time you told a lie?"

Eve raises her wrist as if she's wearing a watch. "Shit... what time is it?"

Cherise smacks her friend on the shoulder, laughing.

"Naw. Seriously," Eve says, "probably a month ago."

"What was the lie?" Cherise asks.

"Nothing major. Mom asked if I remembered to do something she needed me to do, and I told her I did. It was a good thing she called, which reminded me."

Cherise looks at me. "Truth or Dare?"

"Truth."

"Is anybody gonna choose Dare?" Eve says.

"What was your most embarrassing moment during sex?"

"Cherise! We just met her. You can't be asking the lady anything like that!"

Cherise looks at me, shame on her face.

I laugh. "It's okay."

"We can skip it," she says.

"It's fine."

Eve says, "If I were you, I would turn right around and ask her ass the same question... since she wanna get all personal."

"I can't think of an embarrassing moment to be honest. Maybe the first time I gave head... I gagged. But that's it."

"Your turn, Cherise," Eve quickly says. "Same question."

"I pooted on a guy."

"Oh," I say.

"You did *what?*"

"It was horrible, because I was on top, cowgirl style, so my back was to him. I knew I shouldn't've eaten that broccoli at dinner."

"You nasty heffa!" Eve throws her head back, laughing. "You pooped?"

"No! No, bitch! I said *poot.* Poot! It's different from a fart. A fart is loud and obnoxious. This was just funky wind."

I shake my head. *Oh god. I can't imagine that happening to anyone. Poor guy!*

"What did he say?" Eve asks once her laughing fit has subsided.

"He didn't say anything," Cherise says. "I kept riding like nothing happened. We never mentioned it."

"You've never told me this story," Eve says.

"Duh! Now you know why."

"How long did y'all remain friends after that?"

"I never heard from him again."

Eve screams.

"Girl, hush! You're gonna get us kicked out."

Eve wipes the laugh tears from her eyes. "We might as well go ahead and end the game on that note."

"No. Let's do one more question. Your turn."

"Alright," Eve says. "We need to bring it back to something sane after hearing that mess. This is the last question. And all of us will answer. What is the most hurtful thing you've ever said to someone?"

"You answer first," Cherise tells Eve. "I have to think about it."

"Of course it was what I told my ex-husband. I told him I hope he catches a disease that puts his dick out of service for the rest of his life."

"Dang," I say.

"I'm not proud of that," Eve says. "I'm over it." Then she

laughs. "What about you, Millicent? The most hurtful thing you've ever said?"

I think of Tan and my throat tightens. Suddenly I am a ball of emotions, and I close my eyes to hold back the tears.

A hand lands on my shoulder and the water sloshes as someone moves closer to me. "You okay, Millicent?" Cherise says.

I take a minute, trying to keep it under control. Taking a deep breath, I say, "My sister."

"Is she okay?"

I chuckle nervously, can't believe I'm on the brink of tears in front of these women I've known for all of two days. "Yeah, for the most part," I say, taking another deep breath. "She's leaving her husband, and called me, asking if she and my nieces can come live with me for a while until she gets on her feet. I told her no."

"Is he abusive?" Eve asks.

"No," I say. "Not physically."

"Was there any other place she could go?"

"That's the thing," I say. "I don't know. What's eating me up inside is that I didn't seem to care. Didn't ask." I then tell them about Tan and Darell's relationship over the years, all the threats she's made to leave him, and how she called me from a shopping center parking lot the night before I came on the cruise.

"Well," Cherise says, "it just sounds like she caught you at a time when you weren't ready. I'm sure things would've been different if she'd called you any other day."

"Yeah." My voice cracks. "But how could I do her and my nieces like that? If the shoe was on the other foot, there's no doubt my sister would've been there for me, no matter what she had going on at the time."

They are quiet, as if they, too, think it was a heartless

thing to do, but won't say it out loud.

"But hey... I didn't mean to get all sensitive, babbling about my problems. Y'all don't even know me. This is embarrassing." I swipe my eyes with the heels of my hands.

"Girl, please," Cherise says. "You're fine."

"It's nothing to be embarrassed about," Eve says.

"Thank you both," I say.

Eve leans over and pats me on the back.

"And I just want to give you another thanks. This cruise was my time to get away and be by myself so I can clear my head from all the stress at work and home, but you ladies were so much fun, and I haven't laughed this hard in a long time."

"We enjoyed you, too," Eve says. "But don't make it sound like we won't see each other again. You're from Houston, aren't you?"

Nodding, I say, "I am."

"Cherise lives in Pearland; I'm in Richmond. Maybe we can get together and go out for some drinks or something."

"For sure," Cherise says.

"Alright," I say. "We can definitely do that."

8

cigarettes and milkshakes

I lower my eyes, putting on my saddest puppy dog face. "Will you open the door, please? I *sowwy.*"

"Hell no. I'm still pissed."

"Please!"

Mama cracks up and finally steps back to let me in.

"I've missed you," I say, leaning in to give her a kiss, but she turns away, heading to the living room. "What?" I laugh.

"Don't try to come in here, kissing up to me now. Gon' go on a cruise, don't even invite me, and then wait 'til the last minute to tell me you going. I don't even wanna hear it."

"I brought you something back."

She sits on the couch, arms and legs crossed, trying hard to pretend she doesn't care about what I'm pulling from the bags.

"Auntie Millie!" Dana rushes in from the back room. "How was your cruise?"

I wrap my arms around her. "Hey, sweet pea. I got you something, too." I give them both a bag.

"Aww... Millie, you didn't have to," Mama says.

Dana scrambles down to the floor to open hers.

"It's just a little something," I say, and sit on the loveseat.

"Baby, it's beautiful! I love it." She stands and wraps the sarong around her waist and struts around the living room. "Now I need to go on a cruise just so I can wear it. Thanks for the beach towel, too."

Dana jumps up to give me another hug. "Thanks, Auntie," she says. I kiss her chocolate cheek, and then she skips back to her bedroom with her stuff.

"How was your day at work?" I ask Mama.

"It was all right. They still trying to get me to go ahead and retire. A few other people told me they saying the same thing to them. I know it's just their way of trying to get rid of us old folks, so they can bring some young ones in. Pay 'em less. Y'know...."

"Well... are you gonna retire?"

"Hell no! What I'ma retire for? Just so I can sit around here and look crazy?"

I laugh.

She folds the sarong neatly and set it along with the beach towel on the arm of the sofa.

"Where's Petey?"

"Went to the store to get me a pack of cigarettes. I swear I can't wait 'til he gets his own shit. I told him if he pick me up late from work one more time, I'm putting his ass out."

"Did you tell Tan I was coming?"

"I did. She said she'll stop by as soon as she finish her errands."

"I see her car is gone."

"Uhn-huh. She just picked it up yesterday. Muncho finally got it going for her."

"That's good." Settling back on the couch, I say, "Has she told you where she's staying?"

"She ain't told me nothing. And I've stopped asking."

As if on cue, we hear car doors slam outside, and

seconds later Tan and my nieces walk in.

"Auntie Millie!" the girls scream, and I am smothered with kisses.

"I swear y'all act like I've been gone for a whole year. It's only been a few days." I pass out tote bags again. Dana joins us, and suddenly the room is filled with giddy girl talk as they show off and compare their gifts like it's Christmas morning.

Tan is still standing near the door, so I get up. "This one is for you," I say.

"Thanks," she says, and puts the bag on her shoulder.

"Look, Ma!" My eldest niece, Rain, holds up the red Mexican dress I bought for her.

Tan smiles. "Cute."

"Can I talk to you outside for a minute?" I whisper to my sister while the girls are busy with their bags.

Outside, we lean against the trunk of her car.

"Are you okay?" I ask.

She gives a small shrug.

"Did you go back, or—"

"Hell naw, I didn't go back."

Nodding, I say, "Mama said you wouldn't tell her where you're staying."

"That's because I don't want her lettin' Darell know where I am."

"You can tell me," I say.

"I'm not telling you either."

"Dang, sis! It's like that?"

She cracks a smile.

I lay my head on her shoulder. "I'm sorry, sis," I say. "For being insensitive. I was worried about you all week. You know y'all can come and stay with me as long as you need to."

"Don't worry about it," she says. "We'll be fine."

Petey pulls up in Mama's car. He gets out, grinning ear-to-ear. "Made it back huh, Mill?"

"Yep."

"How was it?"

"Beautiful," I say.

"That's good."

"Well?"

"Well, what?"

"Did you talk to Warren? What did he say?"

"Oh. I couldn't take the job, sis. I'm sorry."

"*What?*"

"He offered it to me, even gave me the pay I asked for, but—"

"Petey Green! What the hell you mean you didn't take it?"

"I thought about it, Mill. I ain't tryin' to pull trash and clean toilets for—"

I pounce on him. "Are you out of your fucking mind?"

Tan starts laughing as I slap Petey over and over, going upside his narrow head.

Then Petey starts laughing. "Naw. Shit. Ouch! I'm playing, sis!"

"Be serious! Did you or did you not take the job?"

"I did."

"When do you start?"

"Monday. I meet him Wednesday morning to fill out the paperwork."

I slap him again for playing around with me.

"Seriously though, Mill," he says, "we had a long conversation. I told him everything about what's going on. He seem like he real good people. He was telling me how he got started and built his company."

"Don't embarrass me, Petey. You better be the best damn custodian he got."

My brother laughs and wraps his arms around my shoulders. "Thanks for looking out for me, sis. I owe you one." Then he plants a wet, sloppy kiss on my cheek.

Cringing, I wipe it away. "You punk!"

"Petey, what's taking you so damn long to bring me my cigarettes?" Mama comes out to the driveway.

"Did you tell Mama?" I ask Petey.

"Tell me what?"

"I got a job." He grins again. "Thanks to Mill."

"Hallelujah," Mama shouts. "It's 'bout got-damn-time. I better be the first person you see as soon as you get your paycheck. All that damn money I've put on your books over the years...." She taps out a Pall Mall from the box.

Petey reaches right over. "Gimme one."

"Me too," Tan says.

A few years ago, I would've been firing one up right along with them. But I'm smoke-free now. It was a vow I'd made to myself for my thirtieth birthday. The smell of them still gets me weak sometimes, but I fight through the cravings. I no longer turn to the nicotine sticks to deal with stress, when I want to celebrate something, or if I'm trying to relax.

* * *

"Warren? How are you?"

"Millicent... you're back. I was just thinking about you."

I remembered his voice was deep, but I forgot *how* deep. Smiling, I say, "Yes. Sorry to call so late, but I was with my family, and we were talking, and.... I promised I would call you when I made it home, so I didn't wanna go against my word before the day is over."

He chuckles. "Oh, that's not a problem. I'm a night owl, so I'm wide awake. The day is just getting started for me."

"Is that right?"

"Yeah. I've never been much of a morning person. I am my best around this time."

"I would probably be a night owl, too," I say, "but the job requires me to work the dreaded day shift."

"Ah, that's right. So you're probably getting ready for bed now, huh? To go to work tomorrow?"

"Well, technically I'm still on vacation. I always take an extra day to regroup, get my mind right for the return." I laugh, and he laughs too.

"I hear ya. Sometimes we need a little extra time."

"Exactly."

We are quiet now, and I'm just sitting here blushing, imagining his beautiful lips and fine body.

"Well, hey... Millicent, I was just about to head out to my favorite deli before you called." He chuckles again, a warm, rumbling sound. "I got the taste for a shake all of a sudden, so...." And he's still rumbling, as if wanting a milkshake is something to be embarrassed about. "Would you like to join me?"

* * *

All I can say is the good Lord took his time when he created this one, because the man is gorgeous.

We're at Katz's in Montrose, and as I approach the booth, he's smiling, I'm smiling, and the two women seated at the table across from him turn to see what he's smiling about, probably sizing me up, deciding if I match him physically, if I'm worthy to be with this hunk, but I don't mind because all that matters is that he's here for me, and as he unfolds himself from the table, standing to his full height, he opens his arms and I gladly step right into the hug.

"It's good to see you again," he says, his voice doing things to me I know it shouldn't, especially since this is our first official get-together.

But the body knows what it wants.

“You too,” I say, and I’m already missing the embrace as his arms fall from around me and he holds out his hand, motioning for me to have a seat, wait until I do, and then slides in across from me. My eyes immediately go to his bald head. No bumps, no dents, no scars. Smooth as an egg.

“Millicent.” He smiles again, then wets his lips. “What kinda name is that anyway? Does it mean something?”

“It’s my grandmother’s name,” I say. I don’t bother telling him how much I hated the name until I was well into my late teens. About the teasing in school, being called *Militant*, or the frustration with having to spell it for someone everywhere I went. “Is there a reason behind the all black?”

He chuckles. The first time I laid eyes on him he was wearing a black polo style shirt and black jeans. Today he’s in a black, long-sleeve Henley T-shirt, black jeans, and black boots. “I get it from my dad,” he says. “Trying to be cool like him.”

“He dresses the same way?”

“All his life,” Warren nods. “And it never dawned on me until one of my friends asked about it when we were in high school. I saw Dad leave the house every day wearing black head to toe, but I didn’t think much about it. So I finally asked him, and he said he did it because he woke up every morning with everything he had to do running through his mind, and that choosing what to wear was one less decision he had to make. Then he said, ‘And because it’s just... it’s just cool, Bud. It’s just cool.’”

“Bud? Is that what he calls you?”

“To this day.” He smiles, the reverence for his pops evident in his eyes.

When the waiter comes we order the famous cheesecake shake—a whole slice of cheesecake blended to perfection, served with whipped cream and a cherry on top. Warren tells her to hold the whip on his, and I order mine with a cup of extra cherries on the side.

"Thanks for helping my brother," I say.

"Hey, don't mention it. He aced the interview fair and square. I let him know I wasn't here to pass judgment. And I also told him that I don't expect him to be with me forever. This is a way to gain security, prove himself. But I have high standards for my staff, and I expect him to show up every day, prepared to meet those standards." Warren rests his arms on the table, lacing his fingers, and I notice the wood beaded bracelet on his left wrist. "He reminds me of my brother to be honest."

"How so?"

"It's taking him a while to get serious about making a life for himself. He's a little special." Warren chuckles.

"There's always one in the family, right?"

"I've done a lot for him, but he'd still rather do things his way. Which is usually not the most honorable."

Our shakes are delivered. Warren removes the straw from his glass, setting it aside on the table. He takes a drink, and then makes a satisfying sound as if he's just had a cold glass of water on a humid summer afternoon.

"For a time I was coming here every night to get one of these. I had to stop before I hurt myself."

"It's very good," I say.

We are quiet for a minute, sipping our dessert.

"So..." he says.

"So?" I say.

"Ready to get back to work?"

"Well, that depends. I may be written-up or, worse, suspended."

His forehead crinkles. "Why is that?"

"I wasn't the most compliant employee these past couple of days."

"Nooo. Really? Are you telling me I've come across a rebellious woman?"

Laughing, I say, "Don't get me wrong… I love what I do, but there needs to be more balance amongst all the coordinators. I can't be the automatic go-to just because they know I'll get the work done. We're expected to be on-call at all times, but there should be some leniency during vacations."

He nods his shiny bald head, no doubt recalling my complaints when I told him about it the night we sat in my office. "I agree on that," he says. "But you know that's how it usually works out. The most reliable people get called first."

"Or the ones most-likely to *not* have the courage to say no."

"So you found the courage this time, huh?"

"And I'm prepared to let my boss know how I really feel if there's a problem when I return on Wednesday."

"That's the way to do it. Don't wanna let them burn you out."

"Exactly. But that's enough about work," I say with a wave of my hand.

He takes a slow sip, then sets the glass down gently. I can't help focusing on his beautiful mouth as he licks away the milkshake caught on his top lip. Smiling, he says, "Are you gonna tell me about the cruise?"

I am immediately transported back to the ship, floating on the ocean, the cool breeze on my shoulders and through my hair as I stroll on the upper deck.

Sighing, wistfully, I begin.

Turn the page for an excerpt from my first novel

Hot August Nights

Overview:
In the midst of losing everything...

It is the worst year ever for Cynthia. Within a span of six months she's lost her beloved townhome, her job as a middle grade schoolteacher, and was betrayed by her longtime partner, whom she believed was destined to be her forever. Hurt, homeless, and confused, Cynthia retreats to her grandmother's house in a small town somewhere north of Houston, Texas seeking solitude to heal her heart, forget about relationships, and plot her next move in life. But what she doesn't expect is a knock on her grandmother's door from a man who's come to interrupt her plans.

sometimes you find love...

Following a bitter divorce, life has returned to the mundane for Holiday, who spends his days working to restore homes around town and his evenings at the lake nearby where he sits and reminisce about the daughter he lost to a terrible accident two years ago. He grieves being part of a family unit, but jumping into another serious relationship is not at the forefront of his mind... until he meets Cynthia.

Under sweltering heat during the last month of summer the two find themselves drawn to each other, burning with a desire that only the other can tame. But is Cynthia willing to go against her plans and start anew with Holiday in a small town? Will Holiday be able to convince Cynthia she came into his life to be more than just his summer pastime?

ONE

"Well, you know how the saying goes. Everything happens for a reason."

Cynthia sighed and shifted in her seat, her tailbone numb from sitting nearly three hours as her friend, Tora, braided her hair in preparation for her summer getaway. "Maybe. But this is definitely the worst year ever."

"Or it could just be a sign that you need to start over in every way."

"It can only get better from here," Cynthia said, trying to sound optimistic even though she was reeling inside.

"So what do you plan to do at your grandmother's house?" Tora stepped back to take a sip from her soda, set the glass down hard on the kitchen counter, then popped her knuckles. She grabbed a section of Cynthia's hair to start the next braid.

Cynthia did not consider herself superstitious, but her grandmother liked to believe bad news came in threes, and she wondered if she was getting a taste of what she meant. The first came when her landlord announced he needed his rental townhome back to house his ailing mother and gave her just thirty days to vacate. Second, the charter school where she had been working as a Social Studies teacher for the past couple years was closing its doors due to someone's mismanagement of the funds. And just when she thought her situation could not get any more desperate, her longtime partner fell weak to temptation and tried someone new.

"Look for a job of course," she answered dryly.

Tora dropped the braid from her hand and walked around the chair to face Cynthia. "Wait. You're not planning to move there, are you?"

Cynthia reasoned her hair would have been completed an hour ago if her friend did not stop every few minutes to do something else: change the channel on the television, go to the bathroom, stop one of the cats from playing between the venetian blinds, make a sandwich, turn off the television to turn on the radio. But Tora was doing something free of charge that normally cost her upwards of two hundred dollars, so she had no mind to complain. "No, but I do have to search for a job every day you know. I can't just sit back and hope the few districts I've submitted my résumé to call me, although that would be nice. I hate the whole process. Completing those long-ass online applications. The waiting. Interviews. I don't even know if I really want to teach anymore."

"Really?" Tora sighed this time. "Sis, now don't go getting all discouraged and what-not. You've always loved teaching. Why the sudden change of heart just because of this layoff?"

"I don't know. Maybe it is time for a change like you said. I've been doing it for nine years. I'm open to trying something new. Maybe something in corporate. Who knows?"

Tora unraveled the braid she'd started only to braid it again. "Well, at least try to have some fun, even though I don't know how much fun there is to have out there in the country. Maybe you will meet a cowboy and he take you out to ride his horse or something."

Cynthia almost choked. "Oh lord, Tora." Their friendship was just a few years old. Tora had moved south from

Pittsburgh seeking warmer weather year-round. A hurricane ran her out of Florida, icy winters ran her out of Georgia, snow ran her out of Tennessee, and so she settled in Houston, Texas where there would be only threats of excessive rain and flooding every one hundred years. They met at Cynthia's favorite local barbecue restaurant. She was passing time reading her book club's latest selection as she sat waiting for her order when Tora walked over, introduced herself, and to tell Cynthia Bernice L. McFadden was also one of her favorite authors. Over talk of McFadden's *Loving Donovan* and chopped beef sandwiches they became friends and Cynthia suggested Tora attend the next book club meeting.

"I'm just saying," Tora continued, "don't sit around and sulk. Didn't you say your grandmother is pretty active there in church events and bingo clubs?"

Cynthia sucked her teeth. "My grandma is in her seventies. Why would I want to hang out with her and her senior friends?"

"Hellooo?" Tora waved her hand in the air expecting Cynthia to see the obvious. "Some of those senior women may have sons. And I'm sure not all of them still drive themselves around. Who do you think is taking them to their church banquets and bingo games?"

"Tora, I need a job. A man is nowhere on the radar right now. And definitely not after what Jonath—" She didn't bother to continue.

Tora picked up her glass, taking a long swig to finish off the cola. She twirled a piece of ice around her teeth. "Well, you know what they say: the best way to get over a man is to get under another one."

"*What?!*"

It was a little after two in the morning when Cynthia finally settled down for bed. Her scalp tight and sore from the eight-hour braiding session, she eased down onto the air mattress, the soft pillow offering little comfort for her aching head. Days were so much easier to deal with than nighttime. The day held many distractions to keep her mind busy and off her current situation—mainly the sunken feeling in her chest that seemed to worsen with each passing day. She believed things would get easier, but Jonathan was always right around the corner of her thoughts, unfolding a chair and taking a seat. Jonathan Blackshire. The man she'd spent the past three years of her life with. The man who'd consumed most of her time. It was the type of love affair most girls dream about: the long courtship beginning with talks over the phone to get to know each other on a base level, then romantic dates to test compatibility, which led to conversations about the other's hopes and dreams for the future and for a deeper relationship, then the decision for exclusivity. Jonathan was kind, attentive, generous. Cynthia had no reason to believe their relationship stood on shaky ground. Sure, they had their share of quarrels in between as most couples do, but nothing significant to cause her to question their status. In him she saw the future. But while she stood rigid in her commitment, defying all the elements that seem to split couples apart, Jonathan got tripped up and fell face first into the lap of another woman.

Cynthia rolled over on her side, taking a deep breath as she did so, trying to ease the feeling in her chest. She could not close her eyes because closing her eyes would only bring forth visions of him. Of them. She considered turning on the music app on her phone, but she was not in the mood for a love song and too sad to be shaken by something more upbeat. The air mattress lay next to the floor-to-ceiling built-in bookcase and on the bottom shelf was Tora's grand collection of magazines—the spines of them face-out so Cynthia was able to see she subscribed to everything from those offering tips on clean eating to creating arts and crafts to how to snag and keep a man. With only slices of moonlight cutting through the blinds and across the bookshelf she lay there counting the number of magazines using only her eyes until the slow tick of the analog clock hanging on the far wall lulled her into a dreamless sleep.

* * *

Cynthia pulled her silver Toyota Corolla into the gas station to fill up. It was the only service station left before she made it to her grandmother's house. On the other side of the highway was the only supermarket within a 15-mile radius where the town could purchase groceries, some clothing, and get an auto oil change. As the gas pumped she pulled out her cell phone, pressing the quick key to dial her grandmother.

"Hello Mama Genie," she said when she heard her grandmother's voice on the other end.

"Oh, hey baby, so you're on your way now, huh?"

Cynthia left Tora's apartment earlier than she initially told her grandmother she would. She couldn't wait to be on the road and out of the city where everywhere she turned only reminded her of Jonathan. "I'm here getting some gas near the grocery store. Is there anything you need before I come?"

"Here?" her grandmother shrieked. "You told me you were gonna call me before you left. The food ain't near-bout done yet. You trying to sneak up on me?" Then she fell into her full-belly laugh, which made Cynthia smile.

"Well, I thought I'd surprise you."

"Good thing I put it on when I did or else I'm sure you would've been starving had I sat here and waited for you to call me." She laughed again. "But naw, I don't need nothing. Holiday come by here about a hour ago and he gon' bring back the salt-bacon for my greens. He should be back pretty soon."

Cynthia heard the snap of the gas pump signaling the tank was full. "Hold on a minute, Mama Genie." She set her cell phone in the passenger seat, hopped out the car to place the pump back in its slot, and grab her receipt. "Who is Holiday?" she asked, placing her key in the ignition and cranking up the car.

"Did I tell you the last time we talked I think some people getting ready to move in the house next door?"

"No, not that I remember," Cynthia said. She usually came down to visit at least three times a year: at Christmas, for Mother's day, and in the summer for her grandmother's birthday. But for the Christmas past Jonathan surprised her with a weekend ski trip to Colorado along with a few of their friends. By May Cynthia was heartbroken and trying to understand what hit her and could not fathom being around anyone—let alone her grandmother who believed Jonathan was the epitome of what she hoped for for her granddaughter and future grandson-in-law—so she conjured up an excuse of why she had to forgo their Mother's day celebration.

"Well him and his daddy been here every day near-bout working on the house. And he come by sometimes to see if I need anythang when they go to town for some supplies."

"Oh, that's really sweet of him."

"Unh-huh," her grandmother continued, "he a real nice young man. His daddy seem pretty nice too. I think his name Frank."

"Well I hope the people moving in are nice. I still miss Sister Dunham," Cynthia said, referring to the woman who occupied the home next to her grandmother throughout her childhood and teen years.

Mama Genie exhaled. “Me, too.”

Cynthia finally pulled out of the parking lot and headed down the road she’d traveled so many times before. The road that led to the place where she could always find peace and solace.

TWO

A blast of heat along with the aroma of southern cooking greeted Cynthia as she opened the screen door to let herself in. “Mama Genie, that oven got it so hot in here! You’ve been cooking all morning or what?” She set her luggage next to the coffee table and stepped into the kitchen to give her grandmother a tight hug and kiss on her cheek, breathing in the familiar scent of Avon’s Skin-so-Soft body oil and Charlie perfume powder. All four burners atop the stove were occupied: a big pot of greens on one of the eyes in the back, whole baby carrots with slices of butter on top and sprinkled with brown sugar simmered next to it, butter beans on one in the front, a skillet of cornbread ready to go into the oven on the other. A pecan pie sat on the counter next to the flour and sugar canisters.

“How you doing, sugar?” Mama Genie turned to smack two kisses on Cynthia’s cheek too. “Everything should be ready in about another hour.”

“No problem. I ate something before I came anyway, so I’m okay for now.” She took a seat at the small table in the kitchen, but got right up because the heat was too much for her in the narrow space. “Why do you have the door open letting all the cool air out? Doesn’t that make the A/C work harder or something?” Cynthia walked back to the living room to close the front door.

“The A/C ain’t on,” her grandmother said.

"Why not? You're not hot in here?" She could already feel sweat pooling in her cleavage.

"It ain't been cooling lately so I just leave it turned off during the day."

"What do you mean it's not cooling?" Cynthia went to the thermostat in the hallway even though she knew looking at the thermostat was not going to change anything. The dial noted it was eighty-three degrees inside. "How long has it been like this and why didn't you tell me? Did you call a repairman?"

"Not yet. It ain't been bothering me none. You know I'm cold-natured and I just turn my li'l fan on at night."

Cynthia pursed her lips. She knew this had more to do with the cost of the repair than her grandmother's preference for lukewarm temperatures—which only served as another reminder of her lack of disposable funds to help out. She decided the repair would be charged to her credit card if necessary and worry about the expense later, but there was no way she was going to let Mama Genie walk around in all this heat. "I'm calling someone to come out and take a look at it first thing tomorrow morning," she told her. "I'll be upstairs unpacking."

The air was even stuffier upstairs and Cynthia opened the two windows of her childhood room. One overlooked the backyard that was not really a backyard but a wide open field of grass and weeds. The other window was positioned on the side and faced the side of the house next door. She looked out at Sister Dunham's old house recalling the many sweet moments she spent sitting on the steps of her front porch as Sister Dunham and Mama Genie sat in the rocking chairs talking about many things. The porch now was built to extend from the front all the way around to the back of the house.

She emptied the clothing from her suitcase onto the floor, separating them into piles to be washed, wanting to get rid of any lingering cat hair picked up from Tora's apartment. Cynthia was draining her meager savings living in an extended-stay hotel when Tora offered her a place to stay in her apartment and set up an air mattress in the den slash home office. She was grateful for the hospitality, but the French doors of the den offered her little privacy, sleeping on an air mattress every day was a drab, Tora liked cats, and they were accustomed to going to the den to relieve themselves. So when Cynthia woke up many mornings to see the eyes of two Blue Point Siamese staring at her through the glass doors, she knew she had to get away for a while to figure out her next move. She'd called her grandmother to tell her she was coming for a month-long visit. Here, she would have a whole room, her own bed, and an environment fresh and free of cat litter.

She took off her clothes, bra and panties, and threw them on the piles, too. In a dresser drawer she found one of her old favorites—a green T-shirt dress—and pulled it over her head, then slipped into a pair of bikini briefs. The dress fit snugly around her hips now and fell just mid-thigh since she'd put on fifteen pounds in the past few months, placing her at an even 175 on her five-foot, four-inch frame. It was the harsh consequence of being an emotional eater. She gathered the braids as tenderly as she could without screaming out loud into a ball on the top of her head, wrapped them with a silk scarf, then descended the hardwood steps in her bare feet for the utility room just beneath the stairs and started her first load of laundry.

"Is there anything you need me to do?" She kissed her grandmother's cheek again just because. Her face was damp with perspiration and Cynthia pulled the strings of hair plastered near her grandmother's eye back behind her ear.

"Not really. Everything pretty much set. Unless you wanna make some lemonade. I think I got some mix in the pantry."

"Okay, I can do that." Cynthia rifled through the shelves of the small pantry until she came across the can of Country Time lemonade mix. She pulled the plastic pitcher from the top shelf, filled it with water from the sink, then grabbed a big mixing spoon from the dish rack sitting on the counter.

"So ain't nobody call you yet?" Mama Genie came over to take a seat at the table, letting out a puff of air as she sat down.

Cynthia scooped the powdered mix, then sugar, into the water and began to stir. She told Mama Genie often there was no need to buy lemonade in the can when the same brand is sold in liquid form, pre-sweetened and ready to serve, but there are many things Mama Genie just won't give up. "No, not yet," she answered.

"And what you plan on doing if they do call you? You got to drive all the way back for the interview? Or can they do that over the phone?"

"Most-likely I will have to drive back, but I don't mind. I don't expect them all to call me at the same time." Cynthia added a little more powder to the water.

Mama Genie peered at the pitcher. "Are you sure you measuring that stuff out right, girl?" The question seemed more rhetorical to Cynthia as she did not pause to give her time to answer, but continued, "You never know. Somebody is sure to call. They always need plenty teachers. How is that Tora doing?"

"She's fine. She was taking the cats out for a walk when I left this morning."

Mama Genie looked at Cynthia to make sure she heard her right. "Taking the cats out for a walk?"

Cynthia laughed. "Yes, she actually puts them on a leash and takes them out for a walk to get fresh air."

Mama Genie laughed at the image. "I ain't never heard of nobody walking a cat. That girl is still crazy I see."

"She does. Well... she does more carrying than walking them, but she takes them out all the time. Those cats are her babies." Cynthia braced herself because she knew what was coming next. Mama Genie'd asked about her job, her friendship, so it was only natural that she would want to know about the other aspect of her life.

"I'm surprised Jonathan let you come down for a whole month by yourself. I thought for sure y'all would've been headed off on another one of y'all's summer vacations."

Cynthia called Mama Genie several times a week to check on her, to chit-chat, and the conversation oftentimes led into talk about her and Jonathan. And over the past few months with the distance and phone line between them she was able to mask the truth and not reveal what was troubling her. She would quickly say things were fine, rehash something Jonathan had said or done in the past for good measure then lead the conversation on to another subject. But standing in front of Mama Genie now she still wasn't ready to talk about him. She didn't want to think about him. She had come to try to forget about him and that's what she intended to do.

"I just told him I wanted to come and spend some time with you since it's been a while. And he's fine with that."

A bashful smirk crossed Mama Genie's face. "Well don't I feel special," she groaned in her playful, sarcastic way.

"Yep," Cynthia said, "and I even brought a couple dresses so I can go to church with you."

Mama Genie sucked her teeth. "Now I know a storm

must be coming soon if you're going to church with me. Reverend Moore still asks about you every now and then."

Cynthia grabbed two lemons from the produce basket and rinsed them to be cut into thin slices. "I like Reverend Moore, but he just goes on and on and on and on. Service starts at ten o' clock and don't end until three. That's just too long to be in church. It was fine back in the day, but I just can't deal with it anymore, Mama Genie. I'm sorry."

"You don't have to apologize to me," Mama Genie scoffed, "he is long-winded but he's letting the Lord use him. And that's just how you new-age folks are. Attention span ain't longer than a minute."

"Well, I just think one-and-a-half to two hours is good enough. That's how long our services are. Pastor Steward is just as thorough and gets it done in less than half the time. Then we have the rest of the day to do as we please." Cynthia dropped the lemon slices into the pitcher and walked over to the refrigerator, placing it in the freezer.

"And that's what's wrong with people today. Can't sit still long enough to reap the benefits of a good lesson. Something solid. Always in a hurry to move on to do something else." Mama Genie leaned heavily onto the table to assist herself to stand. "Girl, let me get to this bathroom before I wet myself. Listen at the door for Holiday," she said as she shuffled down the hall.

Cynthia pulled open the oven door and slid the skillet of cornbread onto the bottom rack. She grabbed the double-folded dish towel her grandmother used as an oven mitt to lift the lid on the roasting pan to peek inside: two Cornish hens surrounded by red onion and gold bell pepper halves sprinkled with thyme. Cynthia had said she wasn't hungry, but just the smell of it made her forget all about the breakfast taco she'd had. She flipped the oven door back up and walked over to the sink to run dish water and wash the dishes sitting there—anything to keep her hands and mind busy.

A feverish knock on the screen door and a gruff voice calling out for Ms. Genie made Cynthia realize she must have been daydreaming as she did not hear anyone pull into the driveway or footsteps across the porch. "Ms. Genie, you in there? I'm back with your bacon." He tapped on the screen door again.

Cynthia snatched the dish towel from the counter, drying her hands as she went to the living room. She pushed open the screen door and stepped out without a second thought.

"Oh," the man said, and Cynthia watched him as his eyes roved over her starting from the top of her head to her feet and then back to the top again. She was just as caught off guard as she was expecting a young teen, but there was nothing pubescent about this guy. He was thick and broad-shouldered. His hair a thick and short textured Afro—as if he just roughed his fingers through it every morning as a means of styling it. Gray sprinkled his goatee. His skin was smooth and as black and lovely as the sky at midnight. A tuft of hair peeked out near the bottom of the V in his T-shirt that stretched across his chest. Freckles of paint splattered his navy blue cargo pants and the tips of his work boots. He held the bacon wrapped in white butcher paper in one hand and a thin classifieds newspaper in the other.

"You must be Frank," Cynthia said.

He flashed a bright smile. "Uh, no, I'm—" He stuffed the newspaper under his left armpit and brushed his hand against his back pocket. "I'm sorry, ma'am," he said examining the palm of his hand, "I would shake your hand but I'm kinda filthy right now. I'm doing some work next door." He gestured his head towards Sister Dunham's old place.

Cynthia smiled. "That's okay."

"I picked this up for Ms. Genie," he said holding the bacon out to Cynthia. "Tell her I will be here for a while if she needs anything else."

Cynthia took the bacon and watched him descend the steps and get halfway across the grassy path before she stepped back into the living room.

"So he made it back, huh?" Mama Genie said, coming up behind her.

"I thought when you told me about Holiday you were talking about a young boy," Cynthia said and walked back into the kitchen. She removed the strip of tan masking tape from the white paper, unwrapping the mass of fatty meat. Mama Genie turned on the faucet and watched her rinse the bacon.

"He is a young man." She set a plate on the counter and Cynthia cut the meat into large chunks before putting them in a skillet to be fried and then dropped into the pot of greens.

"Not that young. I was thinking about a teenager or something when you said he works with his daddy."

Mama Genie waved her off and plopped down in her favorite kitchen chair. "Anybody younger than me is young."

THREE

Emerald greens, sepia browns, and burnt orange were the colors that swirled through Holiday's mind as he sat on the back porch, taking a break from his work. The lady next door was unexpected and he couldn't get the image of her out of his mind. Her doe eyes and full lips. The smooth brown legs underneath the short dress that hugged her curvy frame. He even noticed her toenails painted a warm orange color—a gold ring wrapped around the second toe. Then her nipples. Had he stared? He couldn't recall, but the way they pierced the thin fabric seemed to be reaching out to him. He took a cigarette out of his back pocket and lit it up. He chuckled at himself because he had not even told her his name, did not ask her for hers. He had been coming to the house doing work for several weeks and had never seen her before. Ms. Genie hadn't told him she had a daughter. But why would she? Their conversations were usually short with just exchanges of hellos and small talk about the weather if she happened to be sitting on her porch when Holiday pulled up, or needed something from the store when he pulled out.

FOUR

Cynthia woke up to the sounds of hammering and sawing against wood. She had lain down to take a nap, restless from the early morning three-and-a-half hour drive to her grandmother's house. The windows were open but there wasn't much of a breeze. Her T-shirt was damp with sweat underneath her arms, her thighs too. She flung the sheet to the side and got up, the hardwood floor surprisingly cool against her feet. She could hear dishes rattling in the kitchen and Mama Genie humming a tune when she opened her bedroom door and crossed the hall to go to the bathroom. Turning on the shower head she stepped right into the tub without waiting for the water to warm.

Mama Genie was sitting on the couch watching the four o' clock news when she made it downstairs. She went to the kitchen to make herself a plate—a full plate this time since she had helped herself only to a small portion of the butter beans and a slice of corn bread earlier, deciding to wait until later in the day to eat. But that's how Mama Genie did her Sunday-style cooking. Cynthia called it Sunday-style because, even though it was Friday, and just the two of them, Mama Genie always made a feast early in the afternoon and they would nibble at the food throughout the day and still have enough left over to last a couple days.

"Sister Nash is coming by to pick me up at five. She

want me to go by the nursery with her and want me to see her new flower bed she got. She say she got it fixed up real nice but want some yellow flowers to go with that red brick. Yellow is her favorite color y'know."

Cynthia did not know, but she pretended she did. "Mmm-hmm. But doesn't Sister Nash live in Douglass County? Why is she driving way out here?"

"Chile, I ask her that all the time, but she insist on us riding together. I tell her it make more sense for me to meet her there, but she say she'll come by and get me so I just let her. It save me from driving anyhow. And I think she just like driving. You know she only been driving for about three years."

"Three years?!"

Mama Genie laughed, slapping her knee as she did. "Yeah, I told her I ain't never knowed nobody to wait until they almost seventy to wanna learn how to drive."

Cynthia took a seat at the table, noticing two plates wrapped in foil. "What took her so long?"

"She just say she never really needed to. They always just had one car and her husband did all the driving whenever they went somewhere. She didn't work y'know. And when them children grew up they just drove her around after the husband passed. But she say they got tired of doing that and she got tired of having to depend on them. But ain't that something? Got her license at this age."

"It is."

"See them two plates right there," Mama Genie said. "I want you to take them next door to Holiday and his daddy. I meant to ask him earlier if he said his daddy's name was Frank. Did he say his name was Frank?"

Cynthia shook her head no, her mouth full of carrots so sweet they tasted like candied yams. "He didn't say anything about his dad. He just gave me the bacon."

Mama Genie offered no response and instead squint her eyes at the television and turned the volume up to hear what the news reporter was saying.

* * *

Cynthia heard the music as she walked the short path to the sea green color house next door. She walked up the three concrete steps to the porch and rapped on the screen. There was a white wood rocking bench on one side of the porch, and two navy blue shell-backed chairs on the other side, rusted with water stains in the seats. The hammering inside appeared to be coming from the back of the house. She cupped a hand around her eye and pressed her face to the glass to peer inside when there was no answer. Prince was loudly proclaiming from radio speakers that there was no particular sign he was more compatible with and all he wanted was some woman's extra time and kiss.

She twisted the handle on the door and stepped in.

It smelled like fresh paint. Plastic covered the wood floors and a variety of tools were strewn about. The small boom box sat on the kitchen counter.

She had not been inside the home since the repast dinner following Sister Dunham's funeral nearly a decade ago. Sister Dunham never married and did not have any children and her only brother had come down from South Carolina to lay her to rest. Cynthia realized now how similar the layout of the house was to her grandmother's except this one was a single story. The combined kitchen and dining room set to the left, the living room on the right. One could see straight to the back of the house from the front door via a long, narrow hallway. The front rooms seemed so spacious now that they were empty of all those plants Sister Dunham had. Plants and owls were her favorite things. Cynthia looked around the rooms as though the pots of palms and Birds of Paradise were still there sitting on the floor next to the sofas, snake plants on the coffee table and kitchen counters, baskets of ferns hanging from the high ceilings, ivies in cages with stems that coiled up the walls. She remembered only the plants with names she could pronounce even though Sister Dunham delighted in teaching her the names of the most exotic-sounding ones. And then the owls. She could still see them everywhere. Colorful ceramic ones. Crystal ones. In artwork all over the house. Wall clocks and whatnots. On Sister Dunham's apron and kitchen towels, her tablecloth where her head lay the day she and Mama Genie discovered her slumped over.

He appeared out of the bathroom and stopped short in the hallway when he saw her standing there.

"I'm sorry, but I knocked on the door several times. I guess you couldn't hear me over the music," Cynthia told him.

"Oh. I didn't know," and he took a step forward then stopped again. Cynthia found it charming as he suddenly tried to cover his chest with his hand. He was shirtless.

"Umm, I'm sorry. Had I known you were coming I wouldn't've been walking around like this."

Cynthia shook her head. "It's no problem. I'm the one who just helped myself and walked right on in, so what could I expect?" She noticed his T-shirt then draped over a short step-ladder in the living room. "My grandma sent you and your dad a plate."

He laughed and walked over to the step-ladder, his boots heavy against the wood floor, and swiftly put on the shirt, then to the kitchen counter to lower the volume on the radio. "Oh okay, so Ms. Genie is your grandmother?

She is something else," he said taking the grocery bag with the two plates in it from Cynthia. "I can already tell it's something that'll put me to sleep if I eat it now." He bounced the bag in his hand as if he was calculating the weight of it. Pop is not here with me today, but I sure will take it to him later. Tell her I really appreciate this and thank you."

"You're welcome."

"Oh," he said and stuck out his hand towards Cynthia. "I'm sorry I couldn't do this earlier. And I didn't get your name."

She took his hand and smiled. "Cynthia."

"Cynthia," he repeated.

"And I know you're Holiday."

He nodded. "Yeah, well, it's Mason, but most call me Holiday. It's our last name." He looked at her now noticing the fitted green dress was gone and she was donning something that looked more like a fancy potato sack and wore beach thong sandals on her feet.

"Is it okay if I look back there," she asked him.

"Oh yeah. Go right ahead. I'm just going to put these plates in my cooler here." He walked over to the kitchen and Cynthia walked up the hallway. She looked into the small bathroom. The pink tiles on the countertop and shower walls were being replaced with a light gray marble; the white cabinets replaced with light gray ones. Sister Dunham's old room and the guest bedrooms had been painted white. They used to be shell pink. Then she walked out to the back porch.

"My grandma told me some people were finally moving in here," Cynthia said when she heard him step out onto the porch. "It's been vacant for a long time."

"My Pop's friend bought this a few months back and is getting it fixed up for his daughter he told me. As a graduation gift. She's graduating from college in December I think."

"Oh wow. Talk about a great gift. All I got was a bunch of cards from the ladies at the church—some with a few dollars in them—and my grandmother cooked a big dinner and those same ladies came over to the house and we ate." She laughed.

"Yeah, and he's upgrading everything, too. We just finished this porch here last weekend." He stood beside her and gave the banister a firm shake as if to test its sturdiness.

"It looks nice. Well, I don't want to keep you from your work," she said and descended the steps.

"Oh, it's not a problem at all. It was a welcomed break. Thanks again for the lunch."

Cynthia nodded and waved. And she didn't have to look back to notice that, instead of entering the house through the back door, Holiday rounded the porch on the side and watched her until she disappeared.

FIVE

"Hey, Pop." Holiday called out to his dad as he entered the house. Frank Holiday was sitting on his recliner, his feet propped up with one of his ankles bandaged. He'd stepped in a grassy hole while out giving an estimate on another job site somewhere and twisted it.

Holiday took a seat on the coffee table opposite him. The strong smell of BENGAY was in the air. "So it's not feeling any better today," he asked him, gesturing towards his foot.

"Naw, still pretty sore when I try to walk."

"So you've just been sitting here all day doing nothing?"

"Sitting right here." He looked at Holiday, flashing him a sly smile.

"And you're sure you don't want me to take you to have the doctor look at it?"

Frank shook his head stubbornly. "Nope."

"Ms. Genie sent over a plate for you. She thought you were working today."

"Oh yeah?"

"Yeah, she had her granddaughter bring it. I didn't even know she had a granddaughter. I thought she lived alone. Fine, too."

"Oh yeah?" Frank said again.

"Yep. A beautiful sistah."

"Well, that shouldn't be too surprising. Just look at Ms. Genie. She got a little weight on her, but you can tell she was something tough back in the day. Li'l ol' waistline. Wide hips. Big legs. I can believe it."

Holiday chuckled at this.

"They say the apple don't fall—"

"Too far from the tree," Holiday finished for him, and they laughed.

Holiday stood up and stretched. "Pop, you need anything? I'm about to take a shower then head over to Jesse Lee's. You know it's tournament night. Spades and dominoes."

"It's the last Friday of the month already? Man, time just keep flying."

"Yeah, so I'll be all night. The jackpot's coming home with me this time."

"Oh, that's what I meant to tell you. Annette called and told me to tell you to pick up the boy from his Auntie Roxy's house. She said she had something to do tonight and couldn't."

"She did? Why didn't she call me?"

Frank looked up at him. "She said she called you, but you didn't answer."

"I didn't get a phone call from her." Holiday walked over to the dining table where he'd set his phone and keys. He looked at the phone screen. "No missed calls."

"Hey," Frank said, "I'm just telling you what she told me."

"She did this on purpose. She knew where I was going tonight." He pressed the key to dial Annette. When there was no answer, he hung up and dialed again, this time leaving her a message to call him as soon as she received it. He shook his head and sighed. "Ain't no kids gonna be at the tournament. She know that."

"Son, just bring him by here. I'll look after him and you go on to your tournament."

Holiday dropped his phone back on the table. “Naw, Pop. I’m not going to put him off on you. Especially with your bad ankle.”

Frank said, “It’s all right. We can sit here and watch TV. Play a few games. Maybe I can teach him how to play spades, too.”

“It’s cool. She wants me to watch him, so I’ll watch him.

* * *

Roxy opened the door—a can of Miller Lite in one hand and her twelve-month-old balanced on her hip. “Hey Brother-in-Law,” she said and leaned into him for a hug. “Long-time no see. Where you been hiding?”

Holiday walked past her into the front room, overstepping toys that littered the floor. Her seven-year-old was sitting on the couch sucking his thumb and watching cartoons. He flashed Holiday a silver-tooth smile and waved before turning back to the TV. “I’ve just been working hard. You know me and Pop stay busy out here. If we don’t work we don’t get paid.”

“Uhn huh.” Roxy closed the door. “It ain’t that much work in the world. Why you didn’t come to my birthday party last month? And don’t say you was working ’cause the party didn’t end ‘til damn-near four in the morning. So you still had plenty time to show your face even if your lying-ass really did have to work.”

Holiday just looked at her, wondering why she felt the need to talk to him this way and question his whereabouts as if he was obligated to her. “I just didn’t think it would’ve been appropriate.”

“Appropriate? Look, just because you and my sister ain’t together no more don’t mean you ain’t family. You can still come around y’know? Hell, we ain’t mad at you. Well, Nette is, but that’s—”

He cut her off. "Where is Christian?"

Roxy set the toddler in her crib and she immediately began to cry. "Him and Max just left here riding them bikes somewhere. You know how Max is. He can't wait to get somebody over here he can actually play with." She pointed at her son on the couch. "His ass is just like his daddy was. Lazy. All he wanna do is eat and watch TV all day. I have to *make him* go outside."

"I'm not lazy," the boy said innocently without turning his eyes away from the television.

Roxy sat down on the green sofa, brushed Cheetos crumbs to the floor, and patted the spot next to her. "Have a seat, Brother-in-Law. Why you still standing up? Them boys'll be back soon enough. You want a beer?" She snapped her fingers, "Solone, go get your sister a bottle and Uncle Holiday a beer. Make yourself useful."

"Naw, I don't need a beer and I can't stay," Holiday told her. "Where-bout did they go? I can just go and pick them up and bring Max back here. I'm in my truck."

Roxy slapped the couch again. "*Sit down*, Holiday. Damn. Have a beer with me. Let them kids play. You ain't got nowhere to be. Tell me what's good."

After a six-pack of beer and half a pack of Benson & Hedges shared between them, Holiday left Roxy's around ten with Christian in tow. Roxy just wanted to talk and would not let him leave. She'd put baby Genesis down for bed, made the boys go to their room to play, and turned the television to the oldies music station. For nearly three hours she talked nonstop and Holiday couldn't remember a fourth of what she'd said. Annette had come up in the conversation a few times and Roxy'd tried to convince him that her sister was still very much in love with him, but just had a funny way of showing it sometimes. Holiday decided it was time to leave when Roxy told him he should reconsider and not give up on their marriage. By then Annette still had not returned his calls and forwarded him to voicemail just now as he tried to call her for the seventh time to find out if she wanted him to drop Christian off at her place on his way home.

"So I guess you're spending the night with me, Champ," Holiday said to Christian as he pulled into the driveway.

"Yes!" Christian jumped out of the truck and ran ahead of him into the house.

SIX

Cynthia flipped through the business pages phone book under A/C repair. There was no way to differentiate one good repair service from another, and she figured the ones listed with a big colorful ad were probably the most expensive, so she dialed the first one with only the business name and telephone number listed. She got a busy signal. She hung up and dialed the next one. It rang and rang. She tried another number and the line whirred and buzzed in her ear; it was the business fax number.

Finally her next call was answered.

"Hello, my air conditioner is not cooling. Is it possible to have someone come out and take a look at it today?"

"Hello?"

"My A/C is not cooling," Cynthia said again. "Can someone come out today?"

There were scratching sounds on the other end then the receiver dropped.

"Hello," a woman yelled into the phone. "What you say, honey?"

"Ma'am, can you hear me?"

"Yes, yes, I can hear you now."

"I was wondering if you can send somebody out to check my A/C."

"Check your A/C you said?"

Cynthia said, "Yes, today if possible."

"Okay, sure. What's it doing?"

"Huh?"

"The A/C, dear. What's it doing?"

"It's not cooling."

"Hold on a minute, honey. Let me call my nephew Josh. He's the technician and I don't know what his schedule is like today. He don't like for me to do the scheduling for him no more since he say I overbook him. Hold on a minute."

Cynthia pulled the phone away from her ear as the woman screamed for Josh.

A couple minutes passed before a male voice entered the line. "How can I help you?"

"I was wondering if you can come and take a look at my air conditioner. It's not cooling."

"Yeah? What's it doing," he asked.

Cynthia hung up.

Sister Nash had come by earlier to pick up Mama Genie after she decided the yellow flowers she'd bought yesterday were not enough to spruce up her entire yard and she needed more décor.

So Cynthia had the house to herself again.

She'd brought plenty of things along with her to keep occupied on quiet days like this: word search and Sudoku puzzles, a shoebox full of DVDs she had been intending to watch since last year, the adult coloring book she snagged from Tora's bookshelf even though she did not have anything to color the pages with, and her book club's next pick. She selected the word search book—something light that would not require much concentration—and went out to the porch. It was nearly three o' clock in the afternoon. The sun was bright and high in the sky, the wind nonexistent. Only the hissing and buzz of cicada bugs could be heard since the main road was several hundred feet away and only one car would pass every hour or so breaking the silence.

Sometimes Cynthia missed the simplicity of country life. The spacious solitude. The laid-back friendliness of the townspeople when they came together. Mostly being close to her grandmother. It was her senior year in high school when she decided she wanted to do something different and attend college in the next big city even though she was just miles away from Texas A&M—one of the most celebrated universities in the U.S. She settled in Houston where she attended Texas Southern University's business school, but was soon bored with the classes, yet too far in the curriculum to change majors, so she earned the business degree then decided to try teaching and sought certification through an alternative program. She'd been in Houston ever since and considered herself a city girl now.

But in this still moment it felt like the good old times when there wasn't much to do but she still found joy in doing nothing.

She opened the book to the next empty puzzle and searched for the first word. By her sixth word search she was thinking about him. His smooth dark skin, his wide back, the way sweat glistened on his shoulders, down his chest and stomach. She couldn't resist glancing to her left expecting to see the dark green truck parked in front of the house.

She supposed he took Saturdays off since he had not shown up next door and the afternoon was half-way over. It would make Tora's day if she called to tell her there was a sexy carpenter working on the house next door. Tora would definitely say it was a sign and opportunity for her to forget about Jonathan. Cynthia quickly pushed the thought out of her mind because there was no reason for her to even be thinking about Holiday in that way, or anyone for that matter. It was just a few months ago when her heart was torn in two. The day when she came face to face with what their relationship meant to Jonathan—what *she* really meant to him.

It was the last week in April and, following two days of continuous rain and area flooding, the city was under warning to remain inside unless it was absolutely necessary to be out on the streets. The need to satisfy her craving for Blue Bell's buttered pecan ice cream was necessary enough to be out on the streets after being cooped up in the house for two straight days and she decided as soon as the rain cleared she would go out and feed her sweet tooth. Once inside the store she picked up a half-gallon of ice cream and a few of Jonathan's favorite snacks. When she'd called to tell him she was on her way to see him—because that is how they'd always done it although both had a key to the other's place, they would call to announce their visit and ask if there was anything the other needed—he'd said the area surrounding his house was clear, but the main street at the entrance to the subdivision was blocked due to standing water and she should not try to come—that her 'little Corolla' might get stuck and swept away. And she had laughed and agreed and said she would just go home and see him soon before they hung up. But when he called her back to ensure she was not coming is when Cynthia felt it. That feeling in the gut called intuition. She knew then something was off and so, instead of turning left out of the parking lot of H-E-B to go home, she turned right and headed towards Jonathan's house. There was high water at the entrance just as he'd said and she waited a few minutes until she saw another car make it through the wave before she tried her luck.

Cynthia recognized the SUV as soon as she approached the house. Davina was Jonathan's co-worker and a mutual acquaintance —one that was part of their Christmas ski trip. She stood at the front door to listen for voices on the other side, hoping her intuition was wrong and that there was more than just one coworker inside since it was not unusual for them to get together to watch a game at his place or just sit out on the patio for drinks and chat. Maybe they'd all gotten drunk and ended up having to stay the night to recover but then the storm came.

All was quiet except for the TV.

She contemplated a few seconds whether she should ring the door bell or pull out her cell phone to surprise him and say she was able to make it through the neighborhood. But it was just her way of stalling. Stalling because she needed an answer ready for the question Jonathan was sure to ask, for her reasoning for showing up at his place as if she didn't trust him. Did she trust him? She was sure she did. And it was that trust that made her use the key to let herself in. That trust that made her believe that, despite the opened take-out containers on the coffee table, half bottles of Patrón and wine on the coffee bar, a woman's blouse strewn across the back of the love seat, sandals on the floor, it was all a misconception and Jonathan was just in the office on the computer and Davina was in the bathroom. And Davina would be wearing a tank or undershirt when she emerged because that would be the only purpose for her blouse being on the sofa Cynthia reasoned—a blouse too cute to risk being stained with hot wings sauce.

But Jonathan was not in the office and Davina was not using the toilet. It was the sounds of pleasure that pulled Cynthia towards Jonathan's bedroom. Davina was on her back, her eyes closed and her mouth opened as she hissed and moaned while Jonathan's tongue cleaned her torso.

Cynthia did not shout. She did not scream. She turned and walked out as calmly and as quietly as she'd walked in. But Houston's flooded streets were no match to the tears that poured from her eyes as she drove all the way home.

A set of love bugs floated across Cynthia's view and landed on the page of her magazine, bringing her back to the present. She looked down at them joined together and just as quickly flicked them off with her middle finger. This was the time for her to forget about love and relationships for a while and get used to being free to do what she wanted—to enjoy her own company again. Besides, fine, handsome guys like Holiday usually were either married or had a harem of women.

Cynthia set the Seek-n-Find magazine down and went into the house for the business pages again. She decided she would try one more time for the day to call and schedule for A/C repair in the hopes someone could come out Monday morning.

SEVEN

"I'm sorry, Champ, but I wasn't expecting you here this weekend so ain't no milk for your favorite cereal this morning." Holiday was standing in the kitchen pulling things out of the refrigerator trying to figure out what he could throw together for breakfast. "I can make you a omelet or a grilled cheese sandwich."

Christian was sitting at the dining table, his hand under his chin, trying to decide. "Grilled cheese sandwich, please," he answered, "with mayo."

"Mayo? Since when do you want your grilled cheese with mayo?" Holiday frowned at the thought.

"Since Solone showed me."

"That boy is something else," Holiday smiled. He put the sandwich in a skillet then pulled out another one to make an omelet for himself. Once done, he carried the two plates to the table and sat in the chair next to Christian.

"I still haven't heard from your mama, so I'm not sure what time she wants me to take you home. I had planned on going to this house I'm working on and do a bit of work, but it'll be just my luck she call as soon as we get there and I have to drive all the way back on this side. So we may have to just hang around here until we hear from her."

Christian smacked his lips as he licked butter off his fingers. "Okay. I challenge you to a game of Mortal Kombat."

"Oh I see you begging for another butt-whooping," Holiday swatted at him playfully. "Ready for Kitana to put it on you again."

"No, I'm playing with Kitana this time," Christian said.

"Naw, you can't choose my player just because she's undefeated. You have to play with your own until you become as great as me." Holiday changed his mind when he saw the sunken look on Christian's face. "Alright, I tell you what. You can have Kitana, and I will choose somebody else."

"Okay, good," Christian said, smiling big.

"But, I'm still going to beat you. You know why?"

Christian shook his head apprehensively.

"Just to prove to you that it's not about the player, but about the skills." He patted Christian on the head as he got up from the table to get them something to drink. "You want orange juice or fruit punch?"

"Fruit punch."

Frank entered the room then, walking with a cane. "Whatcha say, *Chris*," he said, squeezing Christian's shoulder as he limped past him to a seat at the table. "You must've snuck in here because I don't remember seeing you last night."

Christian giggled. "*Christian*, Grandpa. You know you have to call me by my whole name. And you was already in the bed."

"Uhn-huh," Frank snorted. "I been calling you Chris since I first laid eyes on you and I ain't about to change just 'cause your mama wanna be acting funny now. You been Chris all your life, but since she going through this change—or whatever it is she claim—she wanna act brand new."

Holiday placed the cup of fruit punch in front of Christian. "C'mon, Pop," he said to Frank. "Don't say things like that. She just want people to call him the name she gave him. She hates nicknames. That's all. She's the same way with her own sister's kids. She tell Roxy all the time what was the purpose of naming the kids what she named them if she wasn't gonna call them that."

Frank said, "Yeah, well, them kids got crazy names anyway, so I would call them something else, too. What are their names? Genevieve? Stallone? Millionaire? What?"

Christian threw his head back in laughter. "Ha! Nooo, Grandpa. It's *Solone* and *Genesis* and *Maximillion.*"

Frank shook his head and laughed. "Exactly. Crazy. Just like I said."

Holiday laughed too. "Pop, you want a omelet? I can fix it for you right quick."

"Naw, I want my plate Ms. Genie sent for me. That's what I want."

"Oh, man," Holiday said. "That was some good eating right there. Wasn't it, Christian?"

"Yep! Real good," Christian beamed.

Frank said, "Is that right?"

"We tore into that when we made it here last night. She sure can cook."

"Ain't nothing like a woman that can cook," Frank agreed. "And you say she got a granddaughter? Is she about your age? Maybe she can cook too." Frank wiggled his eyebrows at Holiday.

Holiday chuckled. "Pop, there you go. Don't even start that."

"What?" Frank said innocently. "I'm just wondering for your sake."

"My sake?"

"Yeah, you been here for several months now. You say you ain't going ba—" He stopped when he saw Holiday shift his eyes towards Christian.

"C'mon," Holiday mumbled. There were a few things Holiday refused to talk about in front of Christian no matter how relaxed and brash in their conversations he and Frank could sometimes get, and his relationship with Annette was one of them.

"I'm just asking for a friend," Frank then said.

"A friend, huh?" Holiday pulled the plate from Ms. Genie out of the refrigerator, removed the foil, and popped it into the microwave.

"Yeah. He seem kinda lonely to me lately and I think he could use a good lady friend. Somebody to talk to sometimes. Spend some time with."

"What makes you think he's lonely?"

"Oh, uh... well, he just don't do too much anymore. Just sit around the house if he ain't at work. Or down at the lake. But that ain't nothing if you ask me. 'Specially for a man his age. How he expect to meet a nice young lady if he don't go out sometimes?"

"How do you know that's what he's looking for though? A lady friend? Maybe he don't have a problem being single?"

Christian said, "Daddy, can I have another grilled cheese sandwich, please?"

"One wasn't enough for you?" Holiday grinned.

Christian shook his head. "I eat two sandwiches now."

"Two?! I just think you're trying to compete with Solone. Keep it up and you will be as big as Solone, too."

"And then I can play football and run over everybody on the team," Christian said.

"No," Frank said, "at the rate you going you won't be able to run at all," and he gently poked Christian in his side with the butt of his cane.

"Yes I will!"

Holiday turned the gas pilot on to warm the skillet again. "Back to this friend though, Pop. Like I was saying, maybe he's enjoying the single life. You know women are hard sometimes."

"Yeah, they can be. But it ain't nothing like having someone by your side. 'Specially a good one. And you're—I mean my buddy is a good guy, and I think he'd make somebody real happy one day. Only if he would give somebody a chance."

Holiday shrugged his shoulders. "You never know. I'm sure he's open to it if a good one come along."

The microwave beeped and Holiday grabbed a fork from the drawer. "Tell me if it's hot enough for you."

Frank dug his fork right into the greens as soon as the plate was in front of him. "It don't even matter. I'm gonna eat it just like this here."

* * *

Holiday pulled into the driveway of the house he used to know as home. It was nearly nine o'clock when Annette had finally texted him that she'd made it home and wanted him to drop Christian off. She opened the door wearing a thick blue bathrobe tied tightly across her waist, her hair pulled back into a sleek ponytail.

"Hey, Mama," Christian said and skipped past her.

Holiday and Annette stared at each other a few seconds, one waiting for the other to say something.

"Annette, what's going on," Holiday finally said, his voice steady and low. "Why are you acting like this?"

She raised a brow, looking up at him. "Acting like what?"

"Come on," Holiday said, disinterested in her mock ignorance. "Why would you do that? Why wouldn't you answer my calls? You know Jesse Lee have the tournament on the last Fridays."

"Mason, I forgot all about that."

He shook his head in disbelief. "You forgot?"

"Yeah. I forgot."

"Okay, even if you did forget why wouldn't you answer my calls, Annette? You know I wouldn't do something like that to you." Holiday slid his hands into his pockets.

"Look, I just needed to get out and have some fun for a while. And you needed to spend some time with him," she said, pulling the robe belt even tighter.

"I have no problem keeping Christian," he told her. "You know that. But how much longer do we have to go on like this?"

"Like what?"

"You just act like you hate me or something."

"Please. Don't start that tonight. You're the one who moved out."

"Well, yeah," he said, "you left me no choice. After what happened with Laila we wasn't even talking to each other. That's no way to live. Christian don't need to be around that."

She raised her voice now. "Don't you even try to act like this was all my fault! I wasn't in this marriage by myself! And what happened to Laila never would have happened if you had just—"

Holiday reached behind her to pull the door close. "Annette, it's been a long time now. We can't keep going through this every time we see each other. I'm living with the pain of losing Laila every day just like you are. But we have to acknowledge the relationship was broke long before that. So can we put all this aside and be friends at least? For Christian?"

Annette stood still, not looking at him, but past his shoulder into the darkness.

It seemed like several minutes passed before she finally said, “I don’t have a problem, Mason. Just be there for Christian, okay?” She backed up into the house, closed the door, and locked it.

EIGHT

"Amen, Amen. Sister Cynthia, let me look at you. It's been a long time. A long time." Cynthia was standing outside Saint Emmanuel Baptist Church with Mama Genie as she did her usual small talk and recap of the day's sermon with the other sisters of the church when Reverend Moore walked up and wrapped Cynthia into a bear-tight hug. "It is so good to see you," he said to her. "So good to see you."

Cynthia stumbled back a little from the pressure once he let her loose. "Good to see you, too, Reverend Moore. How have you been?"

"Ah, Sister, you know I am blessed and highly favored. Can't complain about nothing. God has been so good to me. So good." He dabbed at the sweat that beaded his mouth with his signature white silk handkerchief and Cynthia couldn't help thinking of how, when she attended the church as a teen, the boys joked around and started referring to Reverend Moore as Reverend Catfish, saying his mouth resembled that of a pink-lipped catfish. "Sister Genie told me you was in town and so I made sure to pull out my best sermon just for you. Didn't that sermon touch you, Sister?"

"Of course, Reverend Moore," Cynthia quickly said even though she couldn't even remember the scripture he had been teaching from. She zoned out once he got worked up. And Reverend Moore loved to get worked up. He would strut back and forth behind the pulpit shouting his praises, lean way back and scream his thanks, pause for confirmation from the twenty-three members that his teachings were reaching them as they jumped to their feet and shouted and screamed right back at him to *'Teach, Reverend!'* and *'Say that, Reverend!'*. Tambourines jingled and the organ groaned, which only motivated him to preach some more. Hours more. It wasn't long before Cynthia was tense with a burgeoning headache and just wanted for it all to be over.

"Amen," he said. "You know it wouldn't be right if I didn't spread the good news. The good news!" He leaned back on his heels and Cynthia was sure he was ready to break out into a parking lot sermon, but Mama Genie walked up just in time.

"Cynthia, Reverend Moore is gonna follow us to the house so he can get a plate and take something for Lady Moore since she not feeling well and couldn't make it to church today. Sister Nash is coming, too."

"Amen," Reverend Moore agreed. "I will be right behind you, Sister Genie."

Cynthia said, "Okay, I will go and start up the car."

* * *

Since Cynthia had nothing to add to the conversation regarding the church's upcoming summer revival she retreated to her room upstairs, leaving Mama Genie, Reverend Moore, and Sister Nash in the living room. She changed out of her clothes and lay in bed for a while just staring at the ceiling, then Holiday entered her mind. She was surprised by the jolt of excitement that rushed through her when she noticed his green Chevrolet parked out front as they were driving up the road towards the house. And then she saw him as she pulled into the yard. He was rounding the truck from the other side, his heavy toolbox in one hand. He set the toolbox down and waited as they exited the car before he greeted all of them and thanked Mama Genie on his and Frank's behalf for her generosity and good food. Cynthia had noticed how his gaze lingered on her as Mama Genie told him he was welcomed to come over later for dessert. She could not deny she found him highly attractive as he stood there in the sun, his skin as smooth and rich as a piece of Hershey's Special Dark chocolate.

She shook her head and sighed as if to shake the image from her brain. She picked up the novel sitting on the nightstand. The book club's reading for next month's meeting was a fantasy romance suggested by Tora since it was her time to host. Cynthia figured her imagination didn't stretch far enough to be able to appreciate a tale about a woman wanting to fall in love with a dragon. By chapter three the heroine was dreaming about making love with it.

Cynthia put the book down.

She grabbed her cell phone to check if there were any missed calls or voice mail messages—if a school district had called offering her an interview. Sometimes the mobile signal was poor and the phone would not ring at all, but then she'd notice a missed call when she checked it later. There were none. She then scrolled through the text conversations between her and Jonathan. She scrolled to find the older exchanges. Simple messages like *Babe, let's go to the movies tonight; Me and the crew will be at Julien's after work. You can come if you want; I love you; Do you mind picking up some ice cream on your way; Where did you put the bank card when you came back last night? It's not on the bar.* A few sexy photos were exchanged in between: Jonathan standing in front of the bathroom mirror wearing only a dimpled smile; a teaser of her legs only; a picture of his early-morning erection; a selfie of her lying topless on her back in bed per Jonathan's request. None of it mattered anymore, she thought. He probably had photos of Davina in his phone, too. And God knows what other women. Davina was the project coordinator at National Oilwell Varco where Jonathan worked as a data engineer. She was the only female in their crew and they got together often after work for drinks or sometimes when Jonathan had a backyard barbecue at his house. Davina was tall—taller than Jonathan and all his friends—and model-slim. A brown-skinned, twenty-something from Canada with long, curly black hair. Cynthia had heard the guys joking one time that Davina wasn't much of a looker in the face, but she had a beautiful personality. Even for Cynthia, she was a lot of fun. Davina loved to laugh and she was a major flirt wherever they went. There was never a bar tender or a doorman or a waiter Davina didn't like. Still, for Cynthia she was never a threat. She would see her make playful passes at Jonathan's friends—never Jonathan—and they would just brush her off, blame it on the alcohol, and declare coworkers were off limits. Cynthia tried to think back now if there had been any signs. If there was something she should have seen before that day when she saw Jonathan in bed with someone she knew. Davina wasn't considered a friend per se, but they all hung out together. Davina would sit next to her at these outings or across from her at the table and look Cynthia in the face just the same.

But it wasn't so much that she knew Davina than it was about the boldness of Jonathan. Cynthia could not wrap her mind around his carelessness. She had a key to his place and was free to show up anytime she wanted to unannounced. She could not understand how he could be so relaxed and risk being caught. Did their relationship mean anything to him, she'd wondered that night. Apparently not. Because only a man that didn't give a damn about her would do such a thing. This is what she'd told herself for days after. This is what made her dismiss his phone calls, ignore the knocks on her door for weeks, reject him when he showed up to the school needing to talk and apologize. Cynthia felt there was nothing that needed to be said. Everything she thought she meant to him was void when she stood at his bedroom door and watched him give another woman the same pleasure he'd give her.

Cynthia got up and went to the window when she heard voices outside. She pulled back the curtain to see Holiday standing on the porch next door. He leaned on the banister, resting on his forearms, a cigarette between the fingers of his left hand. Cynthia studied him, watching as he took languid drags of it. *Damn.* Smoking was such an ugly habit, but he was sexy just posed there relaxed and nonchalant. In spite of herself she wondered what was his story. How many women did he have strung along after him? Or was he married? Did he have women strung along while being married? She squint her eyes trying to focus in on his ring finger. It was empty, but maybe he just didn't wear it while working she thought. Reverend Moore and Sister Nash were leaving and he waved goodbye to them. And then, as if he sensed her watching him, he looked right up to her window.

Cynthia jumped back. She stood still a few seconds, holding her breath. Then laughed at the silliness of her reaction. She slid her finger through the split of the curtains and peered out.

He was looking right at her. "Did I scare you?"

Cynthia was caught red-handed. She pushed the window pane all the way up and leaned out. "What you say?"

"I said I hope I didn't scare you."

"No, you didn't scare me. I thought this bug was going to fly in here." She fanned her hand in front of her face to shoo the imaginary pest. It was the best she could come up with.

He smiled, his teeth a brilliant white against his dark skin. Cynthia watched as he stubbed the cigarette out on the porch banister and then walked a few paces over to be even with her window. He didn't just walk, he strolled. His movements were slow and easy, as if there was never a need to rush about anything ever in life. She realized now he even talked slow. Not in a boring, drawn-out way, but a calm and laid-back way. "How was church service," he asked.

Cynthia couldn't bring herself to speak bad about Mama Genie's favorite pastor, so she nodded her head and said, "It was good. Reverend Moore is a special one."

"I liked that dress you had on. You looked really nice. I just didn't wanna say nothing like that in front of Ms. Genie or the reverend."

She blushed. The dress was a two-tone sheath: red at the top, pink on the bottom, a skinny pink belt wrapped around her waist. "Thanks." She waved her hand. "Mama Genie doesn't care about things like that. And the reverend, well, he's dished out his share of compliments, too."

"Oh yeah?" Holiday chuckled.

"Yeah." He leaned down on his forearms again just looking at her. The silence unnerving, so she finally said, "I'm surprised y'all are working today. On a Sunday of all days."

Holiday glanced over his shoulder. "It's just me here today. Pop is at the house resting again. He hurt his ankle so he wouldn't've been able to do too much anyway."

“Oh,” Cynthia said. “I hope he’s all right.”

“Yeah, he say he is. He won’t let me take him to have the doctor do a X-ray though. So we’ll see how it’s doing tomorrow. I’ll tie him up and throw him on the back of my truck if I have to to get him there.”

Cynthia laughed. “That’s a shame.”

“He’s something else. But that’s Pop.”

“So you have to do all the work yourself today, huh?” she asked, just making conversation.

He stood up now. “Yeah, the day does go by faster when he’s here. He like to goof around, so he’s always trying to make me laugh.”

Cynthia said, “That’s good. Sounds like y’all have a good time working together.”

He nodded, “Yeah, we do.”

Cynthia cleared her throat, at a loss for what to say next.

“You can come over if you want to,” he said.

She blinked. “Come over?”

He spread his hands over the railing. “That’s if you want to. I don’t mind the company. I won’t even put you to work. I promise.”

A nervous laugh escaped her throat. “Umm... I don’t know about that.” She looked over her shoulder, inspecting the room to see if there was some cleaning she needed to do instead, if the furniture needed dusting. She looked back at him and he was smiling his charming smile.

He said, “Just thought I’d ask. You never know what you can get unless you ask for it, right?”

Cynthia cocked her head. “And what exactly are you trying to get?” she asked him.

“Some company. That’s all. You seem to be as sweet as Ms. Genie. I’m sure you will make painting these rooms a lot more fun for me."

Now she rested her elbows on the window sill. "So, that's it? You want me to come and watch you paint? Sounds about as exciting as watching it dry." She laughed at her own corny joke.

He dropped his head to hide his own laughter, and then nodded. "Yeah. I'm being honest."

She considered it for a few seconds. Here it is just day two of being home at her grandmother's house where she'd planned to come and escape the heartbreak she'd left back in Houston. This was her time to focus on herself and finally let go and move on from the relationship with Jonathan, but this guy was interrupting her plans. Yet, just looking at him made her feel giddy like a little girl experiencing her first crush with her next door neighbor.

"I may stop by for five minutes once I finish up what I need to do." She didn't have a damn thing to do, but she couldn't tell him that.

"Just five minutes?"

"Hey," she said, "truth is, I don't know you. All I know is you're the guy my grandma says picks up things she needs from time to time when you go to town. So, I probably shouldn't even give you five minutes. Not behind closed doors. All it takes is one minute for—"

He raised his hands in surrender. "You're right, you're right. You don't know me. I don't know what I was thinking."

"Uhn-huh," she said, offering a wry smile. "We'll see."